Claimed by the Dragon

Stonefire Dragons
Book 17

Jessie Donovan

Mythical Lake Press, LLC

Claimed by the Dragon

Copyright © 2025 Laura Hoak-Kagey

Mythical Lake Press, LLC

Print Edition

Cover Art by Laura Hoak-Kagey of Mythical Lake Design

ISBN: 9798891560888

Also by Jessie Donovan

Stonefire Dragons

Asylums for Magical Threats

Blaze of Secrets (AMT #1)

Frozen Desires (AMT #2)

Shadow of Temptation (AMT #3)

Flare of Promise (AMT #4)

Cascade Shifters

Convincing the Cougar (CS #0.5)

Reclaiming the Wolf (CS #1)

Cougar's First Christmas (CS #2)

Resisting the Cougar (CS #3)

Love in Scotland

Crazy Scottish Love (LiS #1)

Chaotic Scottish Wedding (LiS #2)

WRITING AS KAYLA CHASE

(Sexy contemporary romances)

Starry Hills

Want Me Forever

Stay With Me Forever

Marry Me Forever

Trust Me With Forever

The Stonefire and Lochguard series intertwine with one another. (As well as with one Tahoe Dragon Mates book.) Since so many readers ask for the overall reading order, I've included it with this book. (This list is as of October 2025.)

Short stories that lead up to *Persuading the Dragon / Treasured by the Dragon*:

The Dragon Play (Stonefire Dragons Shorts #3)
Dragon's First Christmas (Stonefire Dragons Shorts #4)

Semi-related dragon stories set in the USA, beginning sometime around *The Dragon's Discovery / Transforming Snowridge*:

The Dragon's Choice (Tahoe Dragon Mates #1)
The Dragon's Need (Tahoe Dragon Mates #2)
The Dragon's Bidder (Tahoe Dragon Mates #3)
The Dragon's Charge (Tahoe Dragon Mates #4)
The Dragon's Weakness (Tahoe Dragon Mates #5)
The Dragon's Find (Tahoe Dragon Mates #6)
The Dragon's Surprise (Tahoe Dragon Mates #7)

Chapter One

Grace Butler resisted looking at the door. Again.

The words from a few days ago echoed through her head: *Stonefire will protect you. If you're my mate, they can't take you away.*

Dr. Trahern Lewis might've offered to mate her to keep her and the twins safe, but she didn't think he really meant it. Emotions had been high after her difficult birth, she'd been worried about her babies, and he'd probably just felt sorry for her.

And right now, waiting for a man who'll never show is a cold reminder about why you can never, ever trust anyone. It's just you and the boys now.

Maybe there would be another way for her to stay with Clan Stonefire. Since her children had a dragon-shifter father, they also carried the gene to shift into a dragon, meaning she either had to give them up or live with a dragon clan permanently.

And she refused to give up her twins. They were hers to love and protect. And if she had to do it alone and be a stranger among the dragon-shifters, she would.

The Scottish accent of Dr. Gregor Innes—he was one of the dragon doctors on Stonefire—garnered her attention. "Maybe I should go check on Trahern. He often loses track of time, aye?"

In other words, Dr. Innes was trying to say this was normal. She shouldn't worry.

And yet, Grace hadn't survived on her own since she was sixteen years old by letting her guard down and relying on wishes and hope.

After all, the one time she'd done that, about ten months ago, had ended up putting her in a fucked-up prison where they'd wanted to happily experiment on her sons as if they were lab rats.

Gripping the bedsheet with her fingers, she replied, "Don't try to placate me, Dr. Innes. He obviously doesn't want this, and I'd rather not force someone into it. I don't want my life to become any more hellish than it has been for the last six months."

"Lass..."

The door opened, preventing Dr. Innes from replying. Grace spotted Dr. Innes' mate and fellow doctor, Dr. Cassidy "Sid" Jackson, who everyone called Dr. Sid.

Dr. Sid met her mate's eyes and shook her head.

Just as she'd thought—Trahern had run.

Grace cleared her throat. "Let's forget this ever happened. I need to talk to the Department of Dragon Affairs. If Stonefire doesn't want me, then maybe one of the other UK clans will. It doesn't matter, as long as they keep my sons safe."

Dr. Sid moved to stand next to her bed inside the surgery. "You're welcome to stay on Stonefire, Grace. There are a lot of human females here to help you adjust. Lochguard has some too, but not as many."

Lochguard was the Scottish dragon clan, up in the Highlands. She'd learned about all the UK dragon clans during her recovery, after the birth of her sons a few days ago.

Dr. Innes spoke up. "You don't have to decide now, lass. You haven't even been discharged yet. And most of the human females on Stonefire are determined to visit you, now that you've mostly recovered. You should ask them your questions, aye? I know you have no reason to trust us yet, but I hope with time, you'll give us a chance."

Her first reaction was to say she didn't want any visitors. She just needed somewhere to take her babies and do her best to love and protect them.

Friends had never been easy for her, at least not after her mother had married that arsehole who'd ended up killing her and then himself.

No. Don't think about him. Instead, she focused on the only two people she loved in the world, her boys—Eli and Eddie. From the moment she'd held them in her arms, she'd snapped out of her bleak, soul-crushing depression and found her purpose.

And for their sakes, she would have to learn a lot, and quickly.

Just thinking about them sent a rush of longing through her. "When can I see my babies again?"

Dr. Sid answered, "Soon. We're just running a few last-minute tests."

Since Grace had been drugged and half-starved while pregnant during her imprisonment, the Stonefire doctors had been overly thorough with both her and the boys. Especially since they didn't know if her twins would suffer any aftereffects.

Not for the first time, she wished she could kill the bastard who'd set her on this path. Not that she knew where he was.

Which was part of the problem—he could show up at any time. After all, she knew he'd get a second payment as soon as the dragon hunters had her babies in their hands.

At least they weren't born inside that hellhole. Focus on the good for now. Pushing her anger aside, she replied, "You'd tell me if something was wrong with them, wouldn't you?"

Dr. Sid nodded. "I don't believe in hiding the truth with something so important. But for now, they seem healthy. The extra tests are just a precaution. They should be back in the next hour or so. Did you want us to leave you until then?"

The dragonwoman's to-the-point attitude settled her a bit. "Yes. I'm not as tired as I was, but I could do with a quick nap."

"Then we'll leave you to it."

Just as Dr. Sid and Dr. Innes turned toward the door, it banged open.

And in the doorway stood the dark-haired, brown-eyed dragonman with pale skin who'd offered to mate her.

He was out of breath and ran a hand through his hair and adjusted his glasses before entering the room. His Welsh accent filled the space. "I lost track of the time. But I'm here, so let's get on with it."

At the lack of inflection, not to mention his word choices, a thread of irritation shot through her.

Before the other doctors could say a word, Grace bit out, "No."

He frowned. "No?"

"You clearly don't want this, so leave."

He opened his mouth, closed it, and stared at the wall to her right, avoiding her gaze.

She was about to tell him to leave again when he finally said, "Let me help you, Grace. Once you find someone more suited, you can break the mating and mate someone else. But for now, you need Stonefire's protection."

"Did you just casually ask me to marry you and then divorce you when I feel like it?"

"Mate, to be precise. But yes, that's correct."

She blinked, trying to figure out how the bloody hell to reply to that.

Dr. Trahern Lewis was often consumed and borderline obsessed with a lot of things, but timekeeping wasn't one of them.

And when his stomach had rumbled enough to make his fairly quiet inner dragon grumble too, he'd checked the time.

Only to find he was late. And while he didn't believe in love, let alone that anyone would actually want to put up with him for life, he'd offered to help Grace Butler.

And one thing Trahern took seriously was honoring his word.

So he'd raced down the hall, to Grace's room. Without stopping, he'd barged in and explained his reason for being tardy.

Judging by Grace's furrowed brows and narrowed eyes, she was probably angry at him. Maybe.

And yet, he'd offered her a logical solution, stating how their mating would only be temporary, on her terms. Instead of being glad or enthusiastic, she'd just blinked at him a few times.

His inner dragon stirred and spoke up. *Don't let her go.*

It wasn't the first time his beast had said that to him over the last few days.

However, since his dragon promptly curled into a ball and went to sleep, Trahern didn't even try to get more information. Instead, he walked toward the bed and finally met Grace's eyes.

They were a deep, dark brown, and they searched his own brown eyes. Trahern had never been very good at reading people's emotions—well, unless they were shouting at him—but he sensed she was confused. And while harder to see, she looked a little lost.

He probably only recognized the latter because he often felt that way himself. Few had patience for his obsessions or the need to finish a task before he could move on. His only real friend in the world, Dr. Emily Davies, even struggled sometimes.

However, seeing someone else who felt out of place only made him want to convince her to say yes all the more. Not that he understood why.

So he walked to the edge of her bed, cleared his throat, and stared down at where her dark-skinned fingers played with the sheets. Her hand was so much smaller than his, and he itched to stroke her skin.

Resisting a frown—he'd never wanted to touch someone that way before—he said, "I can help you with more than a place to stay. I know where everything is in the archives, every section of books, and can help you find whatever you need to better understand your children."

Silence.

Maybe she was worried about him trying to assault

her or coerce her. So he blurted, "You also don't have to worry about me wanting sexual intercourse. I'm a virgin and have no need of it."

He ignored Sid and Gregor's gasps—dragon-shifters were usually virile creatures—and dared a glance at Grace's face.

She frowned at him. "Why are you telling me this?"

"To prove I'm the best solution to your problem. I can help you, your children will be safe, and if they ever need medical attention, I will be right there. We're still trying to determine if your captors gave you anything to harm you or them."

Gregor muttered, "Trahern," but he ignored the Scottish doctor. "Will you mate me now?"

After a few beats, Grace replied, "All right. I'll need a lot of help learning about dragon-shifters to help my boys. Plus, having a doctor always there for my babies is what tips me into mating you. So: no feelings, no sex, and no expectations beyond not hurting each other." She put out a hand. "Deal?"

He stared at her outstretched arm. Touching others was not exactly pleasant, and yet he wondered what her skin felt like. As soon as he took her hand to shake, a jolt shot up his arm and ended at his cock.

Her eyes met his and widened again, but this time in surprise. She quickly dropped his hand, and he resisted rubbing his palm against his trousers. He'd learned a long time ago to wash his hands after leaving. Otherwise, people seemed to get upset.

"Then let's do the mating vows. I'll start."

Grace tilted her head. "Now?"

"We only need witnesses and a declaration. Well, and to sign the paperwork. As soon as we do this, I'll ensure the paperwork is completed."

"Okay," Grace replied. "What do we do?"

"Well, I, Trahern Lewis, claim you as my mate. Do you accept the claim?"

"Er, yes."

"Now you say the same, but change the names."

Grace's brows drew together, but she said clearly, "I, Grace Butler, claim you as my mate. Do you accept the claim?"

"Yes, that's it. I'll talk to Bram now."

He nodded at Grace, avoided looking at Sid and Gregor, and walked out of the room, ignoring a flicker of need to stay near her.

But Grace was his mate in name only. Whatever this feeling was, it'd fade soon enough. It was probably just the newness of some female talking to him about something other than science, or not trying to run away from him at the earliest opportunity.

Yes, that was it.

And as he walked toward Bram's cottage, he went through his list of tasks to complete for the day, penciling in a few more to help prepare Grace and her children for their new lives on Stonefire.

Chapter Two

The next two days flew by in a blur as Grace filled out DDA paperwork, took care of her sons, and tried her best not to look at the door and wonder if Trahern would visit.

He'd signed the mating paperwork and provided his mobile number in case of emergencies, but had been busy with some sort of research. In other words, she hadn't seen him since the mating vows.

Which only reminded Grace that she was in this alone, for the most part, and she could never forget it.

After finishing her discharge papers, she stood staring at her twins asleep in a double pram, and uncertainty crashed over her. She didn't know who to ask for directions, let alone where she could go to buy a few necessities, or even where Trahern's cottage was located.

Especially since she was human and didn't know if anyone would even help her.

For the first time, she wondered if it'd been a mistake to say she didn't want to see any of the human women who'd tried to visit her. They could've at least given her a few tips and maybe drawn a map.

Eddie stirred in his sleep, and she readjusted the tiny hat on his head and smiled. He was the fussier of her boys. They were identical, with the same light brown skin, dark eyes, and bald heads. And yet, their personalities were already starting to emerge.

For the time being, she dressed them by color—Eli in blue and Eddie in green—to make her life easier. Yes, the nurses had put a spot of ink on Eli's foot so they could tell them apart. But she liked to think that, as their mum, she should be able to recognize who was who sooner rather than later.

Just as Eddie scrunched his nose again, the door opened. But instead of the medical staff, a short, curvy woman with reddish-brown hair and green eyes entered, smiling at her. Her American accent surprised her as she said, "Hello, Grace. I'm Melanie Hall-MacLeod. And I know you've been turning away visitors, but I insist on helping you settle in a little. I'm one of the few humans to have had twins on Stonefire, so I figured I could give you some tips."

She blinked. Even Grace had heard of the American and her book about dragon-shifters. "Er, hello. I'm Grace Butler—I mean, Lewis."

After walking nearer the pram, Melanie stopped and smiled down at the boys. "I sometimes forget how tiny they are in the beginning. Mine are about to start school soon and aren't very little anymore. My mate seems to think we should have another baby. And while I love children, my daughter, in particular, is a handful. I'm unsure if I need any more chaos in my house."

Grace struggled to reply. The American certainly didn't have trouble sharing personal things, but Grace usually kept everything to herself.

As she tried to think of what to say, Melanie met her gaze again. "Well, enough about my little hellions—who, I love to pieces, mind you—and let's get you settled. Trahern is doing something to help Snowridge, his former clan, and sadly, can't be here himself."

Part of her breathed a sigh of relief because she could put off being alone with Trahern for a while longer. One of the DDA's requirements for matings was that they had to live together to prove it wasn't a sham. Hers was one, of course, but she had no choice but to live with the dragonman to pretend it wasn't.

A dragonman she barely knew.

Tamping down her worries—the last dragonman she'd trusted still made her distrust the rest—she tightened her grip on the pram and replied, "Thank you."

Melanie waved a hand in dismissal. "Think nothing of it. Now, tell me their names and then I'll take you to the clan's shop before heading to Trahern's cottage. You'll need a few things, for sure, and don't worry, Trahern said to put it on his account and he'll take care of it."

The first of many debts to come. Grace didn't like it, not one bit. She'd have to find a way to pay her own way somehow, and soon.

Melanie placed a hand on her arm and said softly, "Let him take care of you, Grace. Dragonmen can get extra grumpy if you don't let them do it at least sometimes. Trahern is a little...different. But he's still a dragon-shifter, and caring for their mates is serious business."

Grace raised an eyebrow. "We're not really mates. I'm sure you know that."

"Hmm. We'll see about that."

Before she could protest, another woman appeared, with brown curly hair, brown eyes, and fair skin. She also had a baby on her hip, who looked like a mini-copy of the woman, albeit with darker hair. She also spoke with an American accent. "Hello! When Trahern told me he had a mate, I had to come see for myself. I'm Kaylee Perry, by the way. My mate is Snowridge's doctor, and he's the reason Trahern isn't here himself. Which is another reason I had to come and help. Nice to meet you! Who are these two cutie pies?"

Melanie had a more calming presence, but Kaylee seemed full of energy. Grace, on the other hand, still struggled to concentrate on anything after her difficult birth since her brain felt like a thick fog. Which meant being social and chatting about little things was hard.

Still, these women had come to help her. So she

touched each of her boys in turn as she said, "This is Eli in blue, and Eddie is in green."

Kaylee picked up her son's hand and waved. "Say hello, Aidan."

Despite all of her uncertainties, Grace couldn't help but smile.

Melanie gestured. "Come on, Kaylee. We need to pick up some things for Grace, and she probably needs another nap. I know I did after the twins were born. Come to think of it, I probably still always need a nap, and I'm not sure what I'm going to do with all the extra free time once the twins are in school."

As they walked, Kaylee laughed. "Between writing more books, changing more laws, and possibly having another child, if your mate has his way, I'm sure you'll keep busy enough."

Their conversation flitted from one topic to the next, and Grace struggled to contribute. After what her stepfather had done to her mother, she'd kept herself apart and had never really had close friends. She'd always thought that isolating herself meant no one else could hurt her.

And yet, as she watched Kaylee and Melanie, she wondered if maybe she'd isolated herself a little too well.

By the time Trahern had solved Maelon's problem and

helped the other doctor with his formula, it was dark outside.

He expected Maelon to leave immediately to check on his mate and son, but the doctor merely stood, stretched, and studied Trahern.

"What?"

The other doctor shrugged. "I never pictured you having a mate, is all."

"Neither did I. But she needed help, and I wanted to give it."

As Maelon studied him, Trahern averted his eyes. While they had discussed formulas, patients, and medical knowledge many times in the past, Maelon had rarely inquired about his personal life. Only after he'd mated Kaylee had he started talking more.

And Trahern wished he'd go back to the old, familiar way.

Maelon spoke again. "Grace has been through a lot, Trahern. I've been helping with some of the others rescued from that place, and whilst she might be one of the lucky ones, it was no less traumatic for her. Maybe at least try to make her feel comfortable in your home."

He frowned. "My cottage is clean and stocked with everything she needs."

"A home is more than some place free of dirt. Especially with newborns. She'll be stressed and worried and exhausted. In short, she'll need help."

He still kept his gaze averted. "I will offer her my

medical services whenever she asks. And she'll have whatever food or things she wants."

Maelon sighed, and Trahern looked over at the other doctor. Maelon shook his head and shrugged before saying, "Just promise to ask me or Gregor for help and advice, if you need it. I know you'll say you can find a book, but some things are learned firsthand. We want to help you and Grace, I promise. So will you do it?"

Since he knew it would end the conversation sooner, he nodded. "Yes."

"Right, well, that will have to be good enough. Now, come on. Kaylee and Melanie helped Grace settle in, but she's been alone for a few hours now. Grace will probably need a break."

"Let me tidy up first. Then I'll go."

Maelon knew him well enough not to suggest Trahern could do it later. Because he couldn't. He'd think about it constantly, until he'd put everything in its place.

So the dragonman said goodbye, and Trahern cleaned up his research space. An hour later, he walked toward his cottage, thinking of everything he'd solved with Maelon.

He was at his front door before he knew it and opened it. Only to be bombarded by crying children and Grace's voice saying, "Please, please, go to sleep. I don't know what else to do. I've fed you and changed you and used all the tricks. I..."

His dragon, which had been quiet most of the day, spoke up. *Go help her.*

He moved to stand in the doorway of the bedroom he'd given to Grace. She stood next to the bassinets he'd put in the room, her hands hovering over each, as if trying to figure out what to do.

The babies cried louder, and he resisted wincing.

Grace finally noticed his presence and met his gaze. Even he could tell she was distressed.

His dragon spoke up. *Ask what she needs. Otherwise, our mate will cry.*

"Do they have fevers? Or, have they started acting strangely?"

She glanced back at her sons. "No. Their temperatures are normal, and they were content until I tried to take a nap." She rubbed her eyes, and her voice was a whisper as she said, "I thought I could handle this. But maybe I can't."

His dragon growled, but Trahern ignored his beast and went to stand next to Grace. He ignored her heat and scent surrounding him—he most definitely didn't want to lean into it—and studied the two babies before snapping the fingers of one hand, then the other, and back again.

Soon the babies quieted as they continued following the sounds. Then he stopped, leaned closer so they could see him—newborns couldn't see very far—and said sternly but quietly, "You have excellent hearing. That means you must listen to your mum and not make her so worried." They blinked at him, so he continued, "And I'm aware you can't understand English yet. However, I've had a long-standing hypothesis that inner dragons understand language much sooner, picking it up whilst in the womb. So maybe your inner dragons will hear and listen to me when I say: help them and help your mother."

The babies continued to blink, although the one dressed in green scrunched up his face as if not liking what he had to say. Trahern continued as if the babe had spoken. "I know everything must be difficult for you, compared to being inside the womb. But now, you must adapt. Your mother has done a lot to keep you, so help her. Having a parent who wants you is something not to take for granted."

As soon as he said the words, he regretted it. Why he was chatty with the babies, he didn't know. Probably because they couldn't talk back and say he was odd.

Memories of his childhood threatened to rush forth, but he pushed them back into his mental box of Things Never to Think About.

He checked the feet of the first babe, saw the ink spot, and then addressed each of the boys in turn. "Elijah, you're the oldest by a few minutes. Set an example for your brother. And Edward, watch out for your brother. I'm told siblings protect each other, so do that. Do you understand?"

The boys just stared at him. If they could make

rational deductions, they probably would've wondered what the bloody hell he was going on about. But that wasn't new.

Grace's soft voice garnered his attention. "Thank you."

He motioned for the human to move her head closer to the bassinets. "A newborn dragon-shifter's vision is blurry far away, but a little clearer close up. They also see little color at this stage. So, bringing yourself closer for now will probably help them start to recognize your face. Although your voice will be the best clue. How did you talk to them in the womb?"

Grace leaned over, her cheek only a few inches from his, but she focused on stroking Edward's cheek. "Quietly. I was afraid someone would hear me in the prison."

Anger suddenly shot through him. "They've been apprehended and sentenced, you know. The main people in charge of that place."

"I know." She quieted as she reached for her other son's cheek before she added, "But they didn't find him."

"Him?"

"The sperm donor."

He resisted frowning. "You mean the male who tricked you?"

"Yes, that bastard is still out there." She cupped the cheeks of each of her babies. "Stonefire won't let him take them away, will they?"

"No, I've said as much."

She glanced at him, and Trahern looked away, to

Elijah's face. After a few beats, she said, "Thank you for your help. But I'm going to try feeding them again and then see if they'll sleep."

"Since there are two, you're following the instructions to supplement with formula as well, right?"

"Yes."

"I know how to prepare a bottle. I can help you."

She stood up, and he followed suit, daring a glance at Grace's profile. Out of nowhere, he wished to smooth back her curly hair, before tracing her cheek like she'd done with the children.

His dragon spoke up. *Yes, I like that idea.*

Trahern took a few steps back and tugged at his shirt. "So, did you want my help?"

Grace searched his gaze and shook her head. "No. I can handle this, but thank you. You'd better sleep whilst you have the chance."

Despite the unusual urge to stay and say he was helping, no matter what, he pushed it aside, nodded, and headed toward his room.

Not that he got much sleep. And not because of the babies waking up crying at intervals, either.

No, after he'd left his father's place at sixteen, he'd always lived alone. It was less stressful when he didn't have to worry about interpreting people's faces and words to try to figure out if they meant what they said.

But now he had three people in his home, and he wondered if he would interpret something wrong or make Grace angry. Because for some reason, he didn't want to upset her.

And when he finally fell asleep, his dreams brought back how at ease he'd felt with his face so close to Grace's. Unlike with most people, she didn't make him nervous.

Which scared him.

Chapter Three

The following morning, when Grace blinked her eyes open against the bright light, her sleep-deprived brain panicked for a second at the unfamiliar room. Was she back in that prison?

Then her eyes fell on the two bassinets next to her bed, and she let out a sigh of relief. No, this was Trahern's cottage, not the prison.

She rose slowly and stared down at her sons, who were mercifully still asleep. While it would be crazy to think Trahern's words had worked, her babies had been more cooperative after his chat. He'd mentioned something about inner dragons understanding language sooner, or something. Was it true? Grace had no idea. From what little she'd known, inner beasts didn't start speaking to a dragon-shifter until they were school-aged.

It was yet another question for her ever-growing list.

So she wouldn't forget, she took out her mobile phone and added it to her notes. Melanie had said that she and some of the other humans would stop by at least once a day to check on her and answer her questions.

While she didn't think their supposed kindness would last, she hoped they would answer enough of her questions to keep her from feeling like she was useless.

Last night had been bad enough. If not for Trahern, she might've burst into tears and sobbed on the floor.

Stupid post-pregnancy hormones. She needed to get a better grip on herself because Trahern wasn't her boyfriend or husband, or in any sort of position that meant she could ask for his help and lean on him. No matter what Melanie said, Trahern wasn't like the other dragonmen she'd met. He was hard to read and didn't broadcast confidence or ego, like the others.

Like the arsehole who'd dropped her off at that prison without a backward glance.

Eddie stirred a little, and Grace raced to the kitchen to fill the kettle and turn it on. Tea would make her feel more human and ready to face the day.

However, before the water boiled, she heard the little sounds that would soon turn into a full-blown cry if she didn't hurry.

Her breasts ached as she rushed into the room, both because they were full and she was sore.

She'd just finished feeding and burping her second son when the doorbell rang. Resisting a sigh, she stood and took Eli with her to open the door. A woman with chin-length blonde hair and blue eyes stood next to a twelve- or thirteen-year-old girl, who looked a lot like the older woman. The woman smiled at her. "Hello. I know we haven't met, but I'm Dawn Chadwick-Whitby, and this is my daughter, Daisy."

Daisy waved. "Hello! I'm human, in case you were wondering. But my stepdad is a dragon-shifter, as are my brothers. They're at home, though. My stepdad thought it would be easier if he looked after the twins whilst we visit. Four babies at once would be a lot, even with me helping."

Grace blinked. "Er, okay."

Dawn said, "Excuse my daughter. She doesn't beat around the bush. At any rate, Melanie told you the human mates would be stopping by, and I volunteered for today. Mel and I are the two humans with twins on Stonefire. Well, I guess you're the third now. But I understand how hard it can be, and frustrating, and how you want to tear your hair out sometimes, and thought I could offer some tips. Daisy is good with babies, too, so she can help entertain them. Speaking of which, who is this handsome fellow?"

Eli cuddled against her chest, his eyes fixed on the little girl as she made funny faces. Grace wondered what her son could see at this young age—probably just a blurry splotch.

Sensing her mind was about to wander, Grace

cupped her son's head and replied, "This is Elijah, but I call him Eli. Edward, or Eddie, is in the other room, and I should check on him before he starts crying again."

"May we come in? You look like you could use a strong cup of tea."

Even though the words were innocuous, her eyes heated with tears. Grace blinked and cleared her throat, determined not to cry. "Yes, please. If it's not too much trouble."

Dawn's gaze turned sympathetic. "Daisy, go make some tea and see what you can find for breakfast."

"You mean I can cook on my own?"

"Yes, you should be fine. But if you burn down the house, you'll be grounded for years."

Daisy rolled her eyes. "I won't burn the house down. I'm very careful." The little girl looked up at her. "Is there anything special you want? I'm a pretty good cook these days, although that's according to my friend Freddie, and he can't even make toast. So I'm not sure how truthful he is. Still, I *can* make toast. And eggs. And bacon. I could try pancakes or muffins, but that might take a while."

Something about the little girl made Grace smile. "Toast, eggs, and tea are fine."

"Right, then I should get started! Just point me to the kitchen."

Grace motioned down the hall, and Daisy dashed inside the room.

It was then that Eli decided to poop, and the diaper turned warm under her palm. He shifted, and Grace sighed.

Dawn scrunched up her nose. "Well, I think it's time to take care of this young man. Would you let me help you?"

The woman put out her arms, and for a beat, Grace hesitated. Dawn added softly, "I can't begin to understand what you went through. But what you might not know about me is that my first husband was a complete arsehole, and I struggled to trust any man for a long, long time. And it'll take time for you as well. However, at least give Stonefire a chance. The people here really do care about each other and offer help with no strings attached. Regardless of the circumstances, you mated Trahern. And so now you're one of us. Let me at least help you with this so you can eat and take a shower. Believe me, it's the small things that help keep you from breaking down and crying. Even with a mate, I still feel that way with my boys sometimes. So, will you let me help you for a bit?"

Grace was a long way from trusting anyone on Stonefire. However, at the warmth and sympathy in Dawn's eyes, she thought maybe it would be okay to accept a little help. Just enough so she could eat, shower, and be ready to face the day.

Plus, she would be in the same house the entire time.

She gingerly transferred Eli over to Dawn's arms. He moved for a second and then went back to sleep.

"Just direct me to where to change this young man, and you can do whatever needs to be done. I'll check on his brother, too."

For a few beats, Grace bit her lower lip and hesitated.

Then Dawn cooed to Eli, took his little hand in hers, and began to sing a soft lullaby.

Before she could change her mind, she pointed to her bedroom. "In there. That's where the boys and I sleep."

Dawn smiled at her. "Take your time, Grace. Daisy doesn't have school, and my mate is working from home. We can stay for as little or long as you like."

Daisy's voice came from the kitchen. "Grace, are you ready for breakfast? It's nearly done!"

Dawn sighed and whispered, "She knows not to shout across the house."

As the scent of toast filtered down the hall, Grace's stomach rumbled. "I'll eat first. I won't be long."

With that, she dashed to the kitchen. Daisy stood at the stove, spatula in hand, dancing in place as she sang, "Cook the egg, cook the egg, but don't overcook the egg!"

Grace smiled and went to stand next to Daisy. "Thank you for making breakfast."

"No problem! I can make a lot of things. My stepdad is a better cook than me, but I'm catching up. He promised to let me help with Christmas Dinner, and I can't wait."

As Daisy went on about all the things she wanted to

make for Christmas, Grace sipped her tea and then ate her eggs and toast. The girl never stopped talking, and yet, she didn't mind. Grace was too tired to be social, and there was something soothing about Daisy's chatter.

When she finished eating and stood, Daisy took her hand in hers and said, "My mum said you can call us anytime for help. I can cook, and she'll change nappies—I hate changing nappies—and help with your boys. I'm convinced they'll be best friends with my brothers one day, even though my brothers are a little older. But I have older and younger friends, so it's not impossible, I think. Anyway, just promise to ask us for help, okay? It can be hard to live with the dragon-shifters at first since some of them are a little suspicious of humans. Not that I blame them, since some humans are horrible people. But still, give them a chance, and then they'll always help you, whenever. I even got the old timers to smile and help with the last human-dragon children's camp. And everyone said that was impossible! What was I saying? Oh, that's right—let my mum be your friend. She wants to."

Daisy finally stopped talking, and Grace said, "I'll try."

"Well, that's a start. Now, let me do the dishes whilst you do mum-stuff. Let me know if you need me to watch the boys. I'm good with babies, I promise."

"Thank you. I'll keep that in mind."

Grace finally went to take a shower. And as the hot water helped ease some of her soreness and tiredness, she thought about Daisy's words. Grace wanted to believe them, to think most would accept her and help her, but she couldn't. Maybe she'd give Dawn and Melanie and some of the humans a chance, but it would be a long while before she could trust any dragon-shifter.

Chapter Four

After finishing his shift at the clinic and cleaning up his office, Trahern walked home, studying the list Blake Whitby had dropped off for him.

Trahern didn't know the other dragonman well, apart from the few times they'd worked together to solve some clan problems. Blake had been a complete recluse before mating the human female named Dawn. Mainly because Blake had a rare genetic condition where his dragon form lacked nearly all pigment, apart from a black spot on his tail. As such, people had gawked at his white dragon, and he'd stayed away.

While he was still a private person, Blake had stopped by the clinic more often after mating his human. The dragonman was good at backwards engineering things used by the dragon hunters and former Dragon Knights, which had been useful for the various devices

Claimed by the Dragon

that shot out darts or whatever full of drugs. Ones Trahern had helped find remedies and counter-agents for.

However, after the end of their meeting earlier, Blake had slid the stack of papers toward Trahern and said, "This will help you take care of your human and her babies."

"I'm a doctor. I know how to take care of babies."

Blake had shaken his head. "Checking their vital signs or blood results isn't the same as raising them. Just take a look. Dawn likes Grace and asked me to help you." He gestured at the stack. "That's my contribution."

Trahern glanced at the top sheet of paper, which had a table of contents broken into sections. It was orderly, with topics grouped together rationally.

In other words, in a way he might be able to understand.

Blake grunted. "Right, well I promised Dawn I'd be back in time for dinner, just in case Daisy burns the food. Text me if you have questions. I can reply in a clear-cut way, with little ambiguity."

Trahern lifted his gaze and met Blake's hazel eyes. "Thank you."

The other male shrugged. "We've both hidden behind science and numbers, using them as an excuse to stay out of the limelight, so I understand you better than most. However, my last bit of advice is to give the human female a chance. Maybe she'll understand you like Dawn did me and make your life so much better."

With that, Blake left before Trahern could lay out all the ways their situations were different. Dawn had been Blake's true mate, for one. And even if Blake were shy, he didn't struggle to read people's emotions and moods like Trahern did.

Not for the first time, he wished Emily had come back so he could ask her a few things. But she was helping Clan Seahaven in Scotland, and he didn't know when she'd return.

His dragon yawned. *You could text her. Or send a lengthy email.*

Ignoring his beast, Trahern continued studying his list right up until he arrived home. Once inside, he heard Grace curse. He rushed to the kitchen, where she stood in front of the washing machine, glaring down at the water and soap bubbles on the floor.

He frowned. "What happened?"

She jumped and then placed a hand over her heart. "You scared me. How are you so quiet?"

Ignoring the question, he went to the machine and turned it off so the water would stop flowing from underneath it. Then he retrieved a mop and began cleaning up.

Finally, Grace spoke. "I'm sorry. I don't know what happened. It filled up fine but then just started leaking everywhere."

He glanced at her and then back at the floor. "It's my fault. The machine has been acting up recently, and I put off getting it repaired. That's why I'll clean it up."

She rubbed her hands against her hips before replying, "If you make a list of things to be done around the house, I can work on doing some of them."

He stopped mopping and briefly met her gaze. "There's no need. I'll take care of it."

Something flickered in her eyes that he couldn't read. Crossing her arms over her chest, she said, "Let me do something, anything, to help because I don't like owing favors."

He frowned. "Favors? What favors?"

She gestured around herself. "The home, food, clothing, and all the things you buy me. It's all a debt, and I don't like being indebted to anyone."

Studying her gaze, Trahern sensed she was upset. Not that he understood why. "I'm your mate. It's my duty. There are no debts to be repaid."

"But I'm not your mate in truth, am I?" She reached out a hand. "Give me the mop."

He moved it away from her. "No. This is my fault. I'll clean it up."

She moved closer. "Trahern, give it here. I made this mess, not you."

As she reached for the mop handle again, she slipped on the soapy water. Trahern moved to catch her, with Grace's front pressing against his. For a moment, she clung to him as her heat and scent filled his nose. She was warm and soft, with a hint of something...like flowers. Leaning his nose to where her neck met her shoulder, he inhaled deeply.

A sense of peace mixed with desire rushed through him.

His dragon spoke up. *She is ours.*

Warning bells rang inside his head, and Trahern focused on moving Grace to the nearest chair. He quickly released her and took several steps back.

She blinked at him, her lovely dark brown eyes making him want to stare into them forever. Normally, he couldn't hold eye contact for long before his skin itched and prickled.

But Grace's gaze made him feel the opposite.

Time stood still as they stared at one another. Then a baby cried, followed by a second, and it snapped Trahern back to reality, and he remembered Blake's list.

"I'll check on them."

With that, he rushed out of the kitchen and focused on checking the twins to see if he could get them to stop crying.

Grace watched Trahern all but run out of the kitchen, and she did her best to catch her breath and slow her racing heart.

One minute she'd been irritated that Trahern wouldn't let her help and earn her keep, and the next she'd been slipping and falling into his arms.

His deceptively strong arms.

For a few seconds, with his arms wrapped around her, she'd felt safer than she had in a long while.

And yet, she wasn't that naïve idiot any longer, the one who trusted a dragon-shifter she barely knew. One who'd ended up getting her pregnant to make some money.

And yes, rationally she knew Trahern wasn't going to woo her with false promises and pretty words to get her into bed. The man was a self-proclaimed virgin, despite him probably being at least thirty years old.

However, she refused to lower her guard. Her sons were her top priority, and she needed to learn everything she could to help them. Anything else was just a distraction.

Grace stood, took a deep breath, and worked on mopping up the worst of the water. When finished, Trahern still hadn't returned, so she went to check on her babies.

She found him sitting in the rocking chair in the corner of her bedroom with Eli in his arms as he recited words that sounded like...the periodic table of elements?

Trahern finally quieted and stared at Eli, who stared back at him. Eddie made a few grunts, and she scooped up her other son. Once she had him cradled in her arms, she looked up to find Trahern staring at her.

His pupils flashed to slits and back. Only once, but she still frowned since she'd never seen his eyes do that. Other dragon-shifters seemed to constantly talk with their inner dragons, but not Trahern.

Before she could think better of it, she blurted, "Do you not like your dragon half?"

He frowned and looked back at Eli. "What do you mean?"

She sat down on the bed, readjusted her hold on Eddie, and replied, "From what I understand, the changing pupils mean you're talking to your dragon half. But if they don't change very often, there has to be a reason. Not liking your dragon half seems the most obvious answer."

He shook his head as he took Eli's hand gently between his fingers. "I don't dislike him. He's just... quiet. That happens sometimes, from what little research I could find. But recently, he's talked more."

"Why?"

Trahern frowned. "I don't know."

Silence fell, and Grace debated asking anything else. She didn't want to give him the wrong idea, that she wanted to get to know him and maybe become mates in truth.

And yet, they were living together, and Trahern was helping with her children.

It's better to know as much as you can now, to better plan the future of your boys. After a deep breath, she asked, "Do you never shift into a dragon, then?"

He remained silent for nearly a minute, playing with Eli's hand, until he finally said, "Only in emergencies, and sometimes not even then."

"Why?"

He rocked the chair a few times before replying, "To change forms requires being in sync with both halves. It takes tremendous effort to get my dragon to stay awake long enough to do it. I usually have to inject a stimulant designed for inner dragons to shift."

"Wait, so is it like you're a diabetic and need insulin? But in this case, you need something to change into your dragon form?"

He finally glanced at her, just for a second, before settling his gaze back on Eli. "Not exactly. I don't have abnormal levels of anything related to shifting into a dragon. At one point, he spoke more to me. But then..."

His voice trailed off, and Grace leaned forward. She shouldn't care, and yet, maybe this would help her sons at some point. Yes, that was why she was so interested.

Ignoring the word "liar" running through her head, she asked, "Then what? Something happened."

"My dragon and I argued."

"About?"

"Sex," he stated.

Grace blinked. "Sex? What are you talking about?"

He took a second before he replied, "Touching others is difficult for me. I can do it for short periods, such as during a medical examination. However, the thought of being naked, touching someone for extended periods, let alone sleeping in the same bed repeatedly, makes my skin itch. I tried to endure it once for my dragon. But as soon as the female tried to touch me, I ended up running away, completely naked, through the halls of the clan, and the rumors spread. Soon, everyone inside Snowridge—my former clan—knew what had happened, and it became a joke. I had been a recluse before that incident, but afterward, I rarely ventured out at all. And then..."

Grace tried to wrap her head around everything Trahern had shared. It took everything she had not to point out he was cuddling her son for an extended period and instead focused on what he'd just said. "And what? Clearly, something else happened."

He rocked, back and forth, for nearly a minute before he finally replied, "My father always had a difficult time with me. My mother died giving birth to me, and my father blamed me for it. Then, when it became apparent that I was...different, he mocked me. And by the time of the botched sexual encounter, he disowned me and left the clan. I don't know what happened to him, and yet, despite how everyone thought I should feel bad, I was relieved. I could focus solely on my studies and didn't have to attempt being a dutiful son to a male who wished I'd never been born."

And just like that, she started to understand Trahern Lewis a little better.

Trahern continued rocking Eli, even though the baby had fallen asleep, and refused to look up into Grace's eyes.

There would be pity or disgust or some sort of negative emotion he couldn't distinguish, anyway.

Although why he'd told her so much, he didn't know.

His dragon spoke up. *She is different.*

For the first time in a long time, he actually replied to his beast, *Why?*

You are drawn to her. You'll figure it out soon enough.

I don't like vague statements.

His beast fell silent and went back to sleep. So he continued rocking, hoping Grace would leave so he could put Eli back into his bed and find someone to repair the washing machine.

However, Grace remained in the room. After she placed Eddie back into his bassinet, she asked, "What do you do for fun, Trahern?"

Frowning, he glanced up for a second. "What?"

She shrugged. "You know, when you're not working or sleeping, what do you do?"

"I read."

"Somehow I don't think it's a cozy mystery with an amateur detective and their trusty cat or dog, is it?"

"Of course not. Recently, I've read some books on theoretical physics to distance myself from work."

Grace smiled for a second, just one, and then turned away from him.

And for some strange reason, he wanted her to turn back around and smile again.

Grace spoke, garnering his attention. "In a few

weeks, once I've healed a little more, maybe we can take the boys to the nearby lake for a picnic."

Her words about healing sent a rush of panic through him. After placing Eli into his bed, Trahern asked, "Are you well? Do I need to fetch my doctor bag?"

She glanced at him. "I'm not about to run any marathons, but I'm fine. Well, except..."

"Except what? You must tell me plainly, Grace. I'm not good at deciphering vague statements."

Looking down at Eddie, she traced his cheek. "Feeding twins has made me sore." She paused before adding, "My nipples are sore. Do you have anything for that?"

Nipples on a female who'd recently given birth were there to provide sustenance for the baby. And yet, Trahern briefly wondered what Grace looked like without her shirt.

Then he pushed aside images of her breasts and cleared his throat. Being around a female so much was addling his brain and probably triggering some dragon instinct to have intercourse and procreate.

Since trying to act on any of those impulses would only embarrass him and make Grace extremely uncomfortable—he'd promised to leave her alone—Trahern moved to the door. "There's something at the clinic. I'll fetch it for you. I'll also get someone to repair the washing machine as soon as possible."

Grace opened her mouth to say something, but Trahern rushed down the hall and out the door.

Although the farther away he got, the more he felt as if he should turn around and go back to Grace.

The unfamiliar feeling scared him, and he debated what to do. Because the only solution he could come up with was to avoid talking with Grace beyond what was necessary. Normally, that was easy for him. And yet, he'd shared more with her today than he had with anyone else. Not even his only friend, Emily, knew as much.

His dragon spoke up. *Don't hide from Grace.*

But Trahern was used to ignoring his dragon, and so he didn't respond. Instead, he focused on finding everything Grace needed to feel more comfortable as a new mother. Then he had one of the young nurses run it over before he sat down and made a new schedule for himself. He needed structured time to help Grace— structured but limited time.

And his task took the entire night, helping him forget about his brief flicker of desire for the first time in his life.

Chapter Five

Over the next month, Trahern avoided Grace. Oh, he visited periodically to ensure she had meals, to ask after any medical concerns, and he'd even hired a young, widowed mother to help Grace with everything related to taking care of dragon-shifter babies.

He'd hesitated about the latter. However, Nikki Hartley-Gray—the second-in-command of Stonefire's security team called the Protectors—had sworn by Helena Westcliff's ability with children. Nikki herself had two daughters, and Helena had helped her for the first few months after she'd given birth the second time. Jane Hartley, Nikki's sister-in-law who was mated to Stonefire's head Protector, had also given Helena a glowing recommendation. The human female had been restricted to bedrest for her highly unlikely pregnancy and had relied on the female as well.

In the end, Grace had seemed to like Helena, which had freed Trahern to work on his latest serums, ones to counteract some of the poisons used by the dragon hunters.

He was in the middle of concocting his latest counter-agent when Dr. Sid knocked and entered without waiting for him to reply. Trahern concentrated on finishing his latest step before looking up at the other doctor.

Over the years, Sid Jackson had earned Trahern's respect. Not only for her intelligence, but also for her common-sense approach to sharing medical knowledge between dragon-shifters. She also kept a cool head under pressure, and had never tried to make Trahern do something he didn't want to, unless it was related to a medical emergency.

However, her usual cool, neutral expression was gone. In its place were rapidly flashing dragon eyes, crossed arms, and a deep scowl.

Instead of trying to figure out what it meant, he merely asked, "What is it?"

"I thought Blake, Gregor, and even Maelon Perry talking with you would be enough. But apparently, with Emily still in Scotland, you have no one to tell you when you're being an idiot. So it's up to me."

"Idiot?" he echoed.

"You're more than aware of how a human female who births a dragon-shifter child has a greater chance of falling into postpartum depression. I know you've read the latest studies, one of which was my own. So tell me: why is Grace sobbing in an exam room, so hard that Dawn and Hayley literally had to prop her up to get her here?"

His dragon became alert, but Trahern focused on Sid's words. "I don't understand. I've asked every morning how she's doing, and she always says she's fine. A few times she's had a headache or a minor medical concern, which I addressed right away."

"Sometimes, people lie to avoid making things difficult, Trahern. If you would've spent any amount of time at home instead of mostly living here, you probably would've noticed how Grace has lost weight, has circles under her eyes, and is emotionally fragile."

Ignoring what felt like guilt squeezing his heart, he replied, "Emotions aren't easy for me, as you know, and it's partly why I hired Helena."

Sid quirked an eyebrow. "Helena sent you loads of text messages over the last two weeks, and you never replied. You also never check in on Grace when she's there, and you don't talk on the phone."

He picked up his mobile and opened the messages. There were over 200 unread ones.

His dragon growled. *Why do you keep ignoring our mate?*

He focused on Sid as he said, "I forget to check whenever I'm working."

Sid growled before saying, "Why did you mate her if you weren't going to help her, Trahern? Someone else would've done it, easily. Grace is a warm but cautious female, who secretly wants to be able to trust and belong somewhere."

He frowned again. "How do you know that?"

"I could overlook you not understanding that part, since my conclusion is from a lot of nonverbal cues. However, I thought giving you the articles about females and depression after birth would be enough. Apparently, it wasn't. So let me state this plainly: Grace needs help. Not in a financial way, as yes, you've done that. But she needs an ally, Trahern. Maybe even a friend. The other human females are trying, but Grace is good at closing herself off. You, on the other hand, live with her. You need to help her adjust to life on Stonefire, help her with dragon-shifters in general, and show her that not everyone is as evil as the male who impregnated her and then turned her in for money. If you're not willing to do that, then maybe I need to talk to Bram about her finding a different living situation, or even a different mate."

His dragon growled. *No. You've ignored me for weeks. Grace is ours to help. Stop ignoring her because she confuses you. Or because you're attracted to her.*

Desire is a distraction. I have more important things to do.

She could be ours forever, if you tried.

Before he could ask for clarification, Sid spoke again. "You always value honesty, Trahern, so please give me the same courtesy and tell me what you plan to do. Are you going to help Grace in all the ways she needs? Or do you want me to find someone else who will? I won't watch her suffer because she challenges your structured, planned-out life."

"What do you mean she's suffering?"

Sid shook her head. "I won't be distracted. What is your decision?"

Studying Sid, he tried to decipher her expression. But it was neutral again, apart from her flashing dragon eyes.

His beast spoke up. *If you abandon Grace, I will never shift again.*

That's unfair. That means people will die.

I don't care. Grace is what you need. What we need. If you toss her away, then you'll lose me too.

Why now? You've rarely spoken up since that one incident with the other female.

I nearly gave up on you. But Grace's presence revived me.

He didn't want to ask, but knew he had to. *Is she our true mate?*

Maybe. I think so. But I'm patient. She just had two babies. I do not need a frenzy. But she is ours. You know my terms.

With that, his beast curled into a ball and ignored him, feigning sleep.

Not that Trahern noticed much since his dragon's words about Grace being their true mate repeated inside his head: *Maybe. I think so.*

The thought of fate determining his future and

changing his ordered life made his heart race and breathing pick up.

He shouldn't have a true mate. As his father had always said, Trahern was incapable of loving or caring about anything but science.

Grace deserved so much better than him.

His dragon whispered, *No. We are also what she needs. Help her.*

Sid leaned down to his eye level, her brow drawing together. "Are you okay, Trahern?"

Without thinking, he blurted, "My dragon said..."

Then he realized what he was doing, and shut his mouth.

Sid's voice gentled. "Grace is your true mate?"

"He thinks so."

She reached out to pat his shoulder but then pulled back, probably remembering how he was different from other dragon-shifters. He didn't revel in touching.

Except with Grace or her boys, he'd never felt itchy or panicky.

The one time he'd held her, she'd made him feel safe and warm and even want to touch her when she was naked.

Dragon-shifters believed a true mate was their best chance at happiness. Not guaranteed—it sometimes went wrong—but better odds than in general.

And yet, as a male who needed science and medicine to order his life, did he really believe in something as unscientific as fate?

His dragon murmured, *What if she's our chance to be happy? To be ours to cherish and take care of?*

Trahern couldn't begin to understand how to cherish someone. He hadn't even noticed signs of Grace's depression.

Before he could continue to talk himself out of anything, Sid said, "I don't usually bring up personal things with you. However, this once, I think I need to. I've heard rumors about what happened on Snowridge, about how your father treated you, not to mention the bullying. And logically, to me, Grace makes a lot of sense for you. She's been hurt, damaged, and needs patience most males couldn't give, I think. But you can. Even if it takes a year or two to earn her regard, I think you could do it. Your case is special, Trahern, and doesn't require jumping into a mate-claim frenzy within weeks or even months. I think if you dared to open up to Grace, you might be surprised and get the future I don't think you ever thought was possible."

He met Sid's gaze and searched her brown eyes before stating, "Grace should have someone normal. Not me."

"You are perfectly normal, in your own way. I have no idea what anyone ever said to you in the past, but you're clever, patient, determined, and one of the most honest people I've ever met. I think a lot of females would love to have a male like that to call their own."

His dragon spoke up. *Go to Grace. She will be even better for us than Emily.*

While he'd always felt comfortable around Emily, he'd never had the desire to touch her or even undress her, like he did with Grace.

For a split second, he imagined Grace smiling at him, touching his cheek, telling him about the latest antics from the twins. And in it, he even smiled back at her.

A feeling he couldn't understand rushed through him—he wanted that more than anything.

His dragon spoke again. *Go to Grace. Open up and the rest will sort itself out.*

He finally glanced at Sid again. He could still say no.

And yet, the image of him smiling with Grace lingered.

Could he care for someone and have them care about him, all without Trahern driving them mental and making them run for the hills?

Someone else knocked, and Gregor poked his head inside. "She's getting worse, Cassidy. You asked for me to wait before doing anything. Can I give her a sedative now?"

The thought of Gregor touching Grace made him growl. Both Sid and Gregor blinked at him.

Trahern stood. "I'll go to her."

Gregor arched an eyebrow at Sid, and the female doctor nodded. "I think he's best for her."

"Aye, well, then come on. Grace is going to make herself sick if we don't do something soon."

Trahern followed the other doctor out of the room and said to his beast, *This better not be a mistake.*

It won't. Just stop holding back with Grace. That's all I ask.

Grace hiccuped from crying so much. It was ridiculous really, as knocking over a glass of orange juice had sent her into a series of sobs that she hadn't been able to control.

She barely remembered Dawn and Hayley helping her to the clinic, or Dr. Sid examining her.

Even now, Hayley sat beside her, rubbing her back, and saying, "Shhh, Grace. Whatever it is, we'll help you."

The other woman had also been imprisoned in the same building as Grace, albeit briefly. At first, she'd avoided Hayley, thinking seeing her would only remind her of that horrid place.

However, once she'd come over and chatted about everything and nothing, she'd realized her mistake and had tried to make friends. Well, to the best of Grace's ability, given how she struggled to trust anyone.

And between Dawn, Hayley, and Helena Westcliff, Grace had been managing.

Or so she'd thought until spilling orange juice had sent her over the edge.

As her hiccups slowed, exhaustion mixed with

hopelessness washed over her. Could she do this? She loved her sons and wanted nothing but the best for them. However, she was starting to think maybe they deserved a home with two people to love and care for them.

Naively, she'd thought Trahern would be there, given how much he'd cooed over her sons—in his unique way—in the beginning.

But after nearly four weeks of him rarely showing up, she'd given up hope he wanted anything to do with her or the boys.

After a knock, Dr. Innes walked in, followed by... Trahern?

She frowned. Staring at him, she demanded, "What are you doing here?"

Trahern's pupils flashed a few times, which confused her. His dragon didn't talk to him. Right?

Dr. Innes cleared his throat. "Trahern wants to chat with Grace alone, Hayley."

Hayley glared at Trahern, but the dragonman never took his gaze from Grace.

And she almost swore determination and concern flared there.

Which was ridiculous. Trahern didn't care about her. Well, beyond the duty of giving her a place to live.

Hayley turned toward her. "Do you want to see him? If not, I'll chase him away."

Trahern said, "I'm not leaving until I talk with Grace."

Her head spun, but whether from exhaustion or Trahern's unusually firm tone, she didn't know.

Maybe she was dreaming. Yes, that would explain Trahern's flashing eyes, long eye contact, and steely tone.

Just as she tried to make her brain work and formulate a reply, Dr. Innes spoke again. "Hayley, come on, lass. It's my professional opinion that they need to talk."

Hayley looked back at her. "What do you want, Grace?"

What she wanted was a lack of cynicism, to erase the months spent inside that prison, and to not worry about her boys ever being taken away from her.

Yet, as she glanced at Trahern again, something seemed different about him. Enough that she replied, "I'll talk to Trahern."

"I'll wait right outside the door. Shout if you need me."

She attempted to smile at Hayley, but didn't quite manage it. "Thank you."

The other woman patted her arm. "Anytime. That's what friends are for."

Friends. How she wished she could embrace it and not constantly worry she'd be tossed aside or used for some sort of machination.

Hayley glared at Trahern before following Dr. Innes out of the room, leaving her alone with her mate, in name only.

As he continued to stare at her, Grace resisted fidgeting. "What do you want?"

He took two steps closer. "I'm sorry."

She frowned. "For what?"

"For not realizing you needed help. That you're exhausted, struggling, and in need of a partner."

"We're not really partners, Trahern," she said softly.

He moved to the drawers on the side of the room and rummaged inside them as he said, "I have trouble reading emotions. Which means you need to state things honestly for me."

Blinking at the abrupt change in subject, she asked, "Pardon?"

Retrieving what he needed, he turned back to her with a syringe and vial in hand. "Unless I've known someone a long time, I can't tell if you're upset or irritated or sad. Well, if someone starts crying or shouting, then I can. But I don't read emotions in eyes or facial expressions as easily as some. So until I know you better, and can memorize your emotional patterns and responses, you have to state plainly what you're feeling. And since you've said fine, I accepted that. But you were lying."

As he filled the syringe, Grace whispered, "I suppose I was."

"No, you were. Because you're not fine."

He walked over, raised his hand, and for the briefest second, traced near her eye. The touch was gone before she could blink, but her skin still tingled from the contact.

Trahern added, "So will you be honest with me? I

mean brutally honest. Politeness will make things difficult, and I won't be able to take care of you properly."

For a split second, a yearning crashed over her. To have someone always at her side, to lean on and help in return, to have someone love her for her, and not abandon her for someone else.

But that was a fantasy, and she only had herself to rely on. Yes, maybe he'd temporarily help her since she'd had a breakdown. That surely didn't reflect well on him, as her mate. But once things were normal-looking again, he'd retreat back to his experiments and laboratory, and she'd be on her own again.

Still, she was tied to this dragonman—at least for now—so she replied, "I will try to be honest. I'm not used to speaking plainly or freely, though. So I might forget sometimes."

His eyes found hers again, and his pupils flashed a few times. "So are you fine?"

It was harder than she thought to murmur, "No, I'm not fine."

He nodded. "Then you need to tell me how to help after I give you this shot. It's something I devised, to help human mothers nursing dragon-shifter babies. It should help raise your energy levels and help with your depression."

She watched Trahern as he administered the concoction, barely registering the prick of the needle. He was intense, focused, and she wondered what it would feel like to be on the receiving end of such scrutiny.

Maybe his focus and determination would translate well into other parts of their lives.

Such as being naked and in bed.

No. She wasn't going to allow her thoughts down that path. He might be handsome with his dark hair and eyes—not to mention his deceptively strong, lean arms—but Grace was done with men, human or dragon. Her sons were all that mattered.

After he disposed of the syringe, he stood in front of her and asked, "What can I do to help you?"

"I-I don't know." He frowned, and she added, "I'm not being vague or polite. I'm always tired, and yet, I don't trust anyone else to watch my boys alone, unless it's Dawn and Daisy."

"Not even Helena? Or me?"

She picked at her jeans. "Helena has helped, but I still don't know her well. I think I only sort of trust Dawn and Daisy because of Daisy—she's still a child, which means she's more honest and straightforward."

"Being honest and straightforward is my specialty."

Did Trahern sound almost petulant?

Surely not. Still, she glanced up and noted he looked off to the side again. Normally, she'd drop it or make a sarcastic remark. However, that wouldn't work with the dragonman. She remembered his words: *"So will you be honest with me? I mean brutally honest."*

Taking a deep breath, she decided to see if he really meant it. "But you're not as honest as you think you are."

His eyes shot back to hers. "What do you mean?"

"Why have you kept away, Trahern? Because if you were as open as you believe, you would've at least told me why you needed space. I don't begrudge you the distance since this isn't a real mating. However, you ran away and hid, and that's another form of dishonesty."

As the seconds ticked by in silence, Grace waited to see if Trahern really wanted the truth from her or not.

Chapter Six

Trahern frowned as he digested Grace's words, and his dragon spoke up. *She's right. I know sharing things is difficult, even with me. But she needs us, all of us.*

I can't share everything at once. She will get frustrated or laugh at me.

Father's words were bullshit, and untrue. I wish you would've listened to me.

Ignoring his beast, he glanced at Grace. She plucked at her top and bit her bottom lip, clearly not at ease.

His dragon sighed. *Say something.*

Unable to maintain eye contact—he didn't want to see her frown or roll her eyes at him—he cleared his throat and said, "I learned a long time ago to keep to myself, as a kind of protection."

"Why? From what?"

Such simple questions with such difficult answers.

Trahern rearranged some supplies on the nearby counter as he said, "My father."

He heard Grace shuffling, and he glanced at her from the corner of his eye. As soon as he did, she tilted her head and said, "I kind of did the same thing—hid myself—because of my stepfather. So I understand."

Just imagining someone trying to hurt Grace made his fingers curl into fists. "What did he do to you?"

It was her turn to look away, toward the floor. "My father died when I was little, and my mum struggled. She thought having a man around would solve everything and went from one to the other. Until *him*." She paused, took a deep breath, and added, "He beat her. And every time, my mum made up an excuse, and I could never convince her he was anything but her protector."

He turned toward Grace and took a step closer. "Did he touch you?"

She shook her head, her curly hair bouncing. "No. As soon as he tried, I ran away. And because of me, my mum..."

Her voice cracked, and Trahern knew something must be wrong. He moved closer. "What happened to your mum?"

"He killed her and then himself."

Bloody hell. Self-absorbed as he was, Trahern rarely wondered about other people's difficulties with their parents. Grace had seemed so...normal.

His dragon spoke up. *Everyone has a past.*

Given Grace's words "because of me," he suspected she felt guilty. Which was rubbish. He stated, "That was not your fault."

Lifting her head, Grace met his eyes again. "I shouldn't have abandoned her. If I hadn't run, he probably wouldn't have done it."

"Maybe, maybe not. But he would've hurt you. Your mother made her choice when she gave excuses and refused to leave. By doing that, she put you in danger."

"It's not that simple, Trahern. Everyone has their own struggles and ways of coping. I suspect from what little you've shared, you keep to yourself as a way of dealing with some inner demons. With what, I'm not exactly sure. However, my mother was the same. She so desperately wanted to be loved that she put up with anything to think she was."

"Perhaps. But you were the child, and she was the parent. It wasn't your job to take her place, allowing your stepfather to abuse you, so she could be spared a little. A difficult choice, yes. But if you'd stayed, he might've killed you, too."

She searched his gaze. "Maybe. I still miss my mum, though."

Before he could think better of it, he blurted, "I didn't know mine. She died giving birth to me, which I was blamed for, as I've mentioned before."

Frowning, she shook her head. "It's unfair to blame a

child for being born. Your mother chose to bring you into the world."

"My father didn't want children. However, I was the result of the mate-claim frenzy, and my mother convinced him to let her keep the child. He'd just found his mate, didn't want to deny her, but then nine months later she was dead. Because of me."

"And your father treated you horribly, didn't he? Long before the incident you shared."

He readjusted his glasses and studied his fingers, unable to maintain eye contact. Trahern rarely talked about his father with anyone. Only Emily knew a little, and the few people on Snowridge who'd witnessed his father's outbursts.

His dragon spoke up. *She is our mate. She deserves to know. Especially since she just told us about her mother, which had to be difficult.*

He blurted, "He told me I was strange, odd, and a disappointment. That I wasn't worth my mother's death. And for many years, he kept me in our home, hidden, so I wouldn't embarrass him further. I learned to keep to myself. It was easier that way."

"Bastard."

Looking up at her harsh tone, he asked, "Pardon?"

"Not you, but your father."

Trahern shrugged. "He was correct on some fronts, though. I'm not like most other people, be it human or dragon-shifter. I *am* odd. But I'm also clever, and decoding complex chemistry problems soothes me. I learned early on that science made sense to me, and found my escape there."

"And that's what you were doing all these past weeks, wasn't it? Escaping into science because it makes sense to you."

After readjusting his lab coat, he nodded. "Yes."

She stood and moved closer. "Were you running from me?"

He met her dark brown eyes again, and the lingering redness and puffiness from crying caused a thread of shame to course through him. He'd done that, by not being there for his mate.

Without thinking, he blurted, "I'm sorry."

"For what?"

"For abandoning you. I feel more at ease around children, so it wasn't your twins. However, you tilted my ordered world, and I didn't know how to handle it. I still don't."

"Well, I'm a little out of place, too, learning about dragon-shifters and how to be a mother, all in one go. How about we just both promise to do our best and be honest? If something frustrates you, tell me. And if I need a short break, maybe you can help me." She put out a hand to shake. "Deal?"

Unlike with most people, he didn't hesitate to take it. He shook a few times, but didn't release her. Instead, he stroked his thumb against the back of her hand and stared at where she continued to grasp him.

The longer her skin was against his, the more his anxiety faded.

"Trahern?"

He looked up. "Hmm? Yes?"

"Whatever you gave me is making me feel a little tired and dizzy. Is that normal?"

"Tiredness, yes. Dizziness might be because you haven't eaten enough. When was the last time you did?"

She frowned. "Yesterday?"

Grace placed her other hand against his chest and closed her eyes. "I don't faint. Ever. And I won't start now."

His dragon spoke up. *Help her.*

"I'll take you home."

Before she could say anything, he swept Grace into his arms. She squeaked and said, "What are you doing?"

"Taking you back to the cottage. I vowed to take care of you, and that's what I'm going to do."

"I'm sure if I sit for a few minutes and drink some juice, I'll be fine."

"No, you need some proper food. Let's go."

Before she could protest further, Trahern exited the room, holding Grace, and marched out into the waiting area.

He barely noticed the stares or Hayley calling him as Grace leaned more against him and wrapped an arm around his neck.

He'd never touched someone for so long, apart from

babies. And yet, there was no panic, no itchy feeling, no desire to drop her off and run away.

She was his responsibility, and she'd run herself ragged because of his neglect.

So from now on, he would make Grace his priority. She'd trusted him enough to mate him and live with him. Now, he needed to be the mate she needed, even if it was going to be the hardest thing he'd ever done.

Chapter Seven

Grace awoke to a male voice saying, "Yes, just like that."

She frowned, then heard Daisy's voice. "You're doing great! Blake's amazing at teaching, even with me. He'll have you cooking in no time so you don't have to always get food from the clan's restaurant."

Cooking? She blinked, trying to make sense of the words.

The last thing she remembered was Trahern carrying her toward the cottage and then...nothing.

My boys. Her breasts ached, and she needed to feed them. But they weren't in their bassinets.

Grace dashed out of the room and headed for the voices in the kitchen. She stopped, seeing Trahern frowning down at the stove as Daisy said, "Try turning it. I'm sure this time you'll get it right."

Trahern muttered, "It shouldn't be this hard. There must be a better, more efficient way to do this."

Blake snorted. "You can figure that out later, I'm sure. For now, flip it over or it'll burn."

As much as she wanted to watch, her gaze searched the room until she found Eddie and Eli in their little bouncy holders, buckled in for safety, asleep.

She debated waking them up, but Daisy saw her and rushed over. "Hi, Grace! Trahern said not to wake you, so hopefully I wasn't too loud. I tried to be as quiet as possible whilst feeding the twins. I forgot how tiny babies can be. My brothers grew so fast, after all."

Even without a cup of tea to wake her up, she managed to follow Daisy's words and ask, "So they've been fed recently?"

"Yes, Trahern took Eli, and I fed Eddie. They're turning into such good little babies. Not fussy at all. Oh, and Trahern is trying to make you breakfast. Isn't that sweet? He apparently can't cook anything, so my stepdad is trying to teach him."

Trahern finally glanced at her and then back to the stove. "Good morning, Grace. If you give me a few more minutes, I should have something edible for you."

She couldn't help but blurt out, "You're learning to cook?"

"Yes."

Nothing else. And yet, she knew he wasn't being rude. No, he was just being Trahern.

She smiled. "Thank you. Give me a little time to pump and I'll be right back."

Before Daisy could offer to help or give her tips—the little girl always wanted to be helpful, no matter the topic—Grace retreated, and by the time she finished, she still couldn't believe Trahern Lewis was learning to cook. To help her.

Maybe he'd meant his vow about taking care of her.

Cynicism crept up, but Grace pushed it down. She'd at least give Trahern a chance. Oh, she wasn't about to fully trust the man and think she could lean on him. But the more she learned about the dragonman, the more she started to understand how difficult this had to be for him.

Mainly because of his father.

So it seemed they'd both had hard times growing up, albeit in different ways.

After tidying up and brushing her teeth, Grace went into the kitchen just as Daisy jumped up with a cheer. "You did it, Trahern! Well done!"

Blake placed a hand on Daisy's shoulder. "Why don't you set the table, Daisy? We'll eat soon."

The little girl dashed to do as suggested, and Trahern turned around, holding a plate full of pancakes. They weren't exactly round, but as the aroma filled her nose and her stomach rumbled, Grace decided she didn't care.

Trahern must've heard her stomach because he frowned at her. "You need to eat."

Her first instinct was to brush it aside and be polite. But then she remembered her promise to be direct, and she said, "I'm less tired but definitely hungry. I could probably eat the whole plate by myself."

Daisy piped up. "There's also fruit and yogurt and some eggs. I don't think you could eat all of that, though."

As the little girl raced to the side and started placing dishes on the table, Grace laughed at the heaping amounts of everything. "No, I don't think I could. Unless there were donuts, then I could probably eat half a dozen of them without thinking."

Trahern placed the pancakes on the table. "I can't make donuts yet, but I can try to learn. Do you know how, Blake?"

Before Blake could answer, Grace shook her head. "No, don't worry about it. I'm sure we can buy some inside Stonefire, for a treat. I'd get sick if I ate them all the time, no matter how good they taste."

"If they make you sick, why would you want them?"

"Haven't you ever eaten too much of something, of a favorite food, and regretted it afterward when you're too full and feel like you'll pop?"

Trahern's brows came together. "No. Why would I?"

Daisy chimed in again. "Because it tastes amazing. Do you have a favorite food, Trahern?"

"I like toast."

Grace blinked. "Toast? That's your favorite food?"

"It was the only thing I could make before, so yes."

She smiled. "Favorite out of necessity. We'll have to change that."

He glanced at her, but didn't smile. She wondered if he ever did.

Trahern replied, "Why? Toast is easy, economical, and nearly foolproof."

Grace opened her mouth to reply, but Daisy beat her to it. "You can still like toast, but maybe there are other foods that can become a favorite, too. Did you have any as a kid?"

For a split second, Trahern focused on arranging the plate of pancakes, rotating it this way and that before he finally replied, "I had ice cream once. I think I liked it, although it was a long time ago."

Knowing more of his history, Grace wondered how he'd gotten the ice cream. She doubted Trahern's father had given him any sort of treat.

Daisy, however, was oblivious to Trahern's past pain and merely said, "The next time we come over, I'll bring some ice cream. What kind? My favorite is cookies and cream. Or fudge brownie. Or chocolate chip cookie dough. Oh, and maybe also rocky road."

Trahern hesitated and then said quietly, "I would like strawberry. That's what I had before."

Daisy scrunched up her nose. "Simple, but if it's your favorite, then that's what I'll get. Now, let's eat! All this talk of ice cream has made me even hungrier."

The little girl sat next to Blake, and Grace sat next to Trahern. As the other pair talked about something to do with their family, Grace leaned over to Trahern and whispered, "Thank you for making breakfast."

"Of course. It should taste fine, even if it's not symmetrical. Next time, I need to improve the shape."

She bit back a smile and loaded her plate with a little of everything before saying, "Some of the best cakes or biscuits I've ever eaten looked awful but tasted brilliant. As cliché as it is, you shouldn't always judge by appearances."

"That's easier for you. If it's supposed to be a circle, it needs to be a circle. Otherwise, it just looks wrong to me."

"Then do this."

She took his plate, cut up the pancake into equal pieces, and pushed it back. "There. Every bit is roughly the same size. Is that better?"

"A little." He finally glanced at her. "Thank you."

As they stared at one another, she wished she could trust Trahern completely. That maybe, just maybe, he would always be honest with her and not deceive or hurt her.

And yet, she'd been burned too recently and might never trust another person with all her thoughts and secrets, let alone her life or love.

Not that she was going to love anyone, apart from her sons.

Thinking of her boys helped her tear her eyes from Trahern's, and she went to work eating her breakfast.

Daisy chattered, filling most of the silence. Maybe

some would find it annoying, but the little girl made her smile and even laugh once. And before she could stop, Grace eventually blurted, "How did you learn so much about dragon-shifters so quickly? It's been less than two years, I think, since your mum mated Blake?"

"Oh, I attended the human-dragon camp before that, and then the plays we performed on Stonefire. But I've always been fascinated and wanted to know more about the dragons. My mum and me are writing some children's books to help other humans understand. Ones that aren't scary or full of lies. I'm sure some will say they're bad books because they show dragon-shifters are a lot like humans—which is true. Apart from changing into a dragon, of course. Mum and I can show you what we have, if you want."

Grace bobbed her head. "I would love to see them, thank you. Maybe we can read the stories to Eli and Eddie." Movement caught her eye. "Speaking of which, Eli wants attention or he'll start crying soon."

She drained the last of her tea and went to her son. Eddie was still asleep, but Eli wiggled and blinked at her. While she'd still be a little blurry at this age, he could see color. And because he was a dragon-shifter, he should be able to see her in detail over the next month.

Regardless, she smiled at her son before kissing his cheek and picking him up. "Hello, little one. Were you a good boy for Daisy and Blake and Trahern?"

Eli moved a hand, and she replied, "Mostly? That sounds about right." She kissed his cheek again. "Let's change your nappy and you can have some playtime on the floor. How does that sound?" He gurgled, and she replied, "I agree, you need loads of playtime to help make things interesting. I'm sure you'll want the noisiest toys, won't you?"

She continued having a one-sided conversation with her son until Trahern stood next to her and said, "We'll take them both to the living room."

After glancing to see Daisy and Blake were gone, she frowned. "When did they leave?"

"Whilst you talked with Eli."

"I should've thanked them, though."

"It's fine. You were smiling, and I didn't want to disturb that."

She readjusted her hold on Eli and glanced at Trahern. But he focused on Eddie, watching as her other son squirmed and started to wake up.

Before she could ask anything, Trahern picked up Eddie, cleared his throat, and said, "Hello, Edward and your inner dragon. It's time for some learning enrichment activities."

Eddie blinked, and Grace laughed. "Just say playtime, Trahern. He's only a month old."

He arched an eyebrow. "His human half won't understand the words for a while yet. However, I think his inner beast is listening. I'd rather help increase his vocabulary."

"You keep mentioning how you think inner dragons understand language sooner. Where did that idea come from? Knowing you, it's based on something tangible."

He turned toward the door. "I'll explain whilst we clean them up."

Once Grace had Eli on the changing table, Trahern spoke up again. "There is a young female dragon-shifter on Clan Lochguard, in Scotland, who has been able to shift into a dragon from a young age, under a year. To shift means you must be able to communicate with your dragon. And the female, Freya Stewart, has continued shifting back and forth for years now. Her parents have let me talk with her, but I haven't been able to get a definitive answer. Maybe when she's a few years older, her inner dragon can tell me how she could shift so young."

"Wait, I thought dragon-shifters couldn't change forms until after six years old or so."

"Normally, yes. That is when they finally emerge from the labyrinth inside a dragon-shifter's mind and have enough courage to start talking. Sometimes it's a little sooner, or a little later. Sometimes, they go silent for self-preservation."

Once Eli was changed and in a new set of clothes, she picked him up and turned toward Trahern. "Yours was quieter before, but not as much now. Why?"

As he fidgeted with Eddie's snaps on his onesie, Grace wondered if she'd gone too far.

However, Trahern murmured, "It's complicated,"

before picking up Eddie and rushing into the living room.

As soon as Trahern fled the bedroom, his beast growled. *Why are you still running and hiding from her?*

He ignored his beast and focused on spreading a blanket on the floor and laying Eddie on the ground. He'd read a few articles about what to do, and so he helped Eddie clap his hands, and then moved his feet, all while reciting some of his favorite theorems. Grace sat on the sofa, Eli leaning his back against her front as she shook a rattle toy.

After a while, Grace finally spoke. "The boys can have some tummy time whilst you tell me why things are complicated with your dragon."

"Why?"

She moved to the floor before placing Eli next to his brother, on his stomach. She replied softly, "I know very little about dragon-shifters, Trahern. I need to learn as much as possible, so I can be there for my sons if they need me. What if they have trouble talking with their inner dragons? Or what if their beasts never come out at all? Or maybe the boys are afraid of suddenly having a second personality inside their heads?"

Glancing over, he saw Grace wringing her hands as she stared at her twins.

His dragon spoke up. *I don't like her being upset.*

He didn't, either. He almost wanted to reach out to her and soothe her.

Not that he really knew how. But he'd seen that with mates or parents with children at the clinic.

Instead, he looked at Eddie and Eli as he replied, "Most dragon-shifters get along with their inner beasts after a few weeks or maybe months."

After a beat, Grace stated, "But not you."

He shook his head. "My father kept me isolated from a young age, when he realized I didn't smile or laugh like most other children. Well, maybe once in a great, great while. But he already resented me for killing my mother, and so he said the deficiency was a good reason to keep me hidden. He told everyone I couldn't handle being around people and that I needed quiet spaces. Which, in part, was true. But..."

He trailed off, struggling to push down the memories of learning about a new medicinal plant he wanted to see. How he'd tried to escape and visit the clan's medicinal garden. But his father had caught him and installed a lock on his door.

On the outside of his door.

His dragon spoke up. *Telling her will help.*

Why?

If she is to be our mate, she needs to understand us. Only then will you eventually accept her.

Before he could reply, Grace's voice snapped him out of his head. "But what?"

At first, he debated sharing more. Grace had been sobbing uncontrollably only the day before.

Yet, as he glanced at her, she stared at him and raised her brows. Then, after a few seconds, she touched his arm. "Tell me, Trahern. Please."

His self-preservation kicked in before he could stop it—which meant deflecting. "It's nothing compared to what you must've endured in the prison."

"Just because we have different kinds of painful memories doesn't mean yours aren't valid, too."

Moving his gaze to where her hand touched him, something shifted inside him. Almost as if he didn't want to hide from her.

His dragon spoke up. *Good. Then tell her.*

Eventually, he cleared his throat and watched the twins again as he said, "When I was a boy, I fell in love with science, specifically medicine and botany." He paused, but then her hand squeezed his arm, and he let out a breath before continuing, "Whilst reading, I discovered a plant that sometimes helped dragon-shifters with anxiety, both with others and with their own inner dragons. I struggled to connect to my beast in the beginning, and I thought maybe, just maybe, this plant might help. Not only could I be more normal, but maybe my father would start treating me like the other boys and girls in my class.

"Snowridge, much like Stonefire, has a medicinal garden. I wanted to see if they had the exact plant and snuck out when my father was out. However, he returned just as I was leaving, and he was furious. My father didn't want others to see his embarrassment, and with my escape attempt, he could no longer trust me to stay put. So, he put a lock on the outside of my door. I spent the next few years alone in my room, apart from school and required clan-wide events."

"Oh, Trahern."

He ignored her soft voice and forced himself to state, "I will never be like him, Grace. I vow it. So even if the boys have trouble with their inner dragons, I will try to help them, in my own way. But I will never call them odd or useless or an embarrassment."

For a few beats, he merely watched the twins squirm on the ground. Then Grace's tight voice demanded, "Is your father still alive? Because I'm tempted to hire someone to find him and lock him in a room for a while to see how it feels."

Her tone was different from its usual lyrical rhythm, so he glanced at her. Grace's narrowed eyes and clenched fists meant she was angry. Probably.

Why, he couldn't fathom. However, he replied, "I don't know. Once he left Snowridge, I never saw him again."

She crossed her arms over her chest. "Well, maybe I'll ask Jane or Ivy to ask their mates to look into it. Did no one think to intervene back in Wales?"

He looked back at the boys, who were trying to lift their heads but not getting far, due to their weak neck muscles. "There was a different clan leader back then, before Rhydian. All he cared about was keeping Snowridge isolated and free of humans. He believed parents should treat their children how they like, as long as they didn't kill or permanently maim them."

"That's horrible."

Grace immediately picked up the son closest to her, Eli, and held him close. She murmured, "Mummy loves you, both of you. No matter what happens, never doubt that."

Eddie made a noise of frustration. Not that Trahern blamed him, considering it was hard work to lift a head at his age.

So he lifted the boy and cradled him in his arms. Eddie blinked at him and fisted Trahern's shirt. "His grip is stronger than average. That's good."

"Trahern."

"Yes?"

"You would never lock the boys in a room like that, would you?"

Something that was almost like pain pierced his heart, which didn't make sense. Nothing was inserted there.

Frowning, he ignored the feeling and replied, "No. I would never lock them in a room and ignore them. I may sometimes get hyper-focused on a task and need to be called several times to get my attention. But it's not deliberate. I have trouble stopping something partway."

Grace laid a hand on his arm again, and some of the

pain faded. She whispered, "I'm sorry. I shouldn't have asked you that."

"Of course you should have. You actually care for your children and want them to be safe. And as you pointed out previously, I ran and hid for weeks."

She squeezed his arm before drawing her hand away.

Part of him wanted to grab it and bring it back.

However, before he could think why, Grace stood. "Do you have to work at the clinic today?"

He also stood. "No. Sid gave me a few days off to ensure you recovered. Do you need another nap?"

After glancing at her, Grace shook her head. "No. But I think we all need a little break from the house and could use a good walk."

"To where?"

She searched his gaze. "That depends. Are you okay with being around a lot of people?"

"I don't seek out large groups. However, I previously stopped by the clan restaurant every day. Short periods of time are fine."

"Well, in that case, there are two shops I want to go to today. If that's okay?"

"Anything you need, Grace. You're mine to take care of."

He nearly blinked. That didn't sound like him.

His dragon spoke up. *She* is *ours to care for, along with the twins.*

Grace's voice was so soft that if he didn't have supersensitive hearing, he would've missed it as she murmured, "And mine to take care of, too. Today I start."

However, before he could ask for clarifications, Grace directed him to a whirlwind of activities. In sixty-seven minutes, they were all dressed, and the boys were tucked into their double-pram. As soon as Trahern locked the front door, he turned around and blinked at Grace's smile. With the sun glinting off her black hair and caressing the dark brown planes of her face, she seemed unreal. If he believed in mythical creatures, he might say she looked like an angel.

He almost frowned at that. What was wrong with him? He wasn't fanciful.

His dragon spoke up. *She is beautiful. It's okay to say and admit it.*

Since doing so might lead to desire again, he ignored his beast and cleared his throat. "Let's begin our walk."

And as he pushed the pram, he silently counted his steps, hoping to clear his confusion and the impulse to take Grace's hand in his.

Chapter Eight

It had taken every bit of restraint Grace possessed not to cry when Trahern had talked about being locked in a room as a child. The thought of him as a little boy, wanting to see some plants and being so severely punished, made her want to do bodily harm to his father.

Although that moniker wasn't right—his sperm donor was more apt.

Grace had her own trauma to deal with, but it was easier to focus on her boys, both the twins and now Trahern. Maybe someday she could share what had happened to her inside the prison. But not yet.

Pushing aside the memories that threatened to break free, she merely enjoyed the sun on her face as Trahern pushed the pram—he'd insisted—and she walked beside him. If nothing else, she wanted to give her dragonman a taste of the childhood he'd never had.

She also burned to know more about her mate. So as they walked, she asked, "How did you end up on Stonefire?"

"They needed help with finding an antidote to something the Dragon Knights had used. Later, Sid asked me to stay to assist with other antidotes and preventative concoctions, and I agreed, as long as most of my time could be spent on research. And with Emily."

"Emily?"

"Yes, she's a fellow doctor and researcher. We met during my time at a university in Cardiff. We worked well together, she wasn't annoyed by my idiosyncrasies, and I didn't mind her questions about dragon-shifter biology. She's human, and didn't know a lot."

For a split second, Grace wondered if Trahern had wanted to mate Emily. However, if the dragonman had known her for so long, then surely he would've asked her by now.

Not your right to be jealous or demanding, Grace. This is a mating of convenience.

Trahern continued, "She's in Scotland right now. I think she may stay there, if I decoded her last email correctly. There's a dragonman she complains about a lot, but then says she looks forward to their meetings. She's usually not so contradictory."

"Maybe she fancies him."

Trahern frowned. "Emily? She has never shown an interest in anyone else since I've known her."

Grace wondered if Emily had wanted Trahern, but

he'd never returned the feeling. Or maybe he hadn't noticed.

And even if she shouldn't ask, she still blurted, "Did you fancy Emily?"

He took a few seconds to gather his thoughts before he shook his head. "No. She's comfortable and familiar, and my only close friend. But I never wanted her to touch me."

Grace frowned. "Do you not like being touched? I'm sorry, I've been doing it a lot, without thinking."

His gaze met hers. "I don't mind your touch."

Time stood still as his pupils flashed a few times.

But then Hayley and her mate, Nathan, spotted them, waved, and came over.

The two dragonmen grunted hellos as Hayley shared some info Grace had asked about earlier. By the time they'd left, Trahern gazed straight ahead, the former heat and connection gone.

She yearned to return to their former conversation about him liking her touch. However, Trahern cleared his throat, pushed the pram, and asked, "Which shops do you need to visit?"

Drop it, Grace. So he likes your touch and not that from his long-term friend. That means little. Besides, this afternoon is for Trahern, and asking him will make him uncomfortable or even drive him away.

After a deep breath, Grace replied as if Trahern hadn't made his earlier confession. "The supermarket, after we stop somewhere as a surprise for you."

"I don't like surprises."

"Normally, I wouldn't spring one on you. However, let me try this once, Trahern. I think you'll like it."

He didn't reply for a long while, and she didn't push. If he truly couldn't handle it, she'd back off.

However, Grace suspected Trahern occasionally needed encouragement to try different things. The experience today should help her better understand how the dragonman interacted outside the clinic or their cottage.

Although she didn't think too closely about why she wanted to know more about him.

"Okay. I trust you, Grace."

His words made her smile. "Thank you, Trahern. I hope I don't fail your trust."

They arrived at a shop that was almost like a newsagent's, but not quite. It had sweets, magazines, a post office counter, and even the latest areas where clan members in their dragon forms could hunt, if they wanted.

However, the small section toward the back was her goal.

The female dragon-shifter running everything smiled at them, her English accented, sounding as if she might be originally from France. "Hello, Dr. Lewis. And this must be Grace. I'm Delphine, and who are these fine young boys?"

The woman's warm smile made Grace want to trust her. Not that she could completely, but she needed to stop treating every greeting as some underhanded scheme to hurt her. "This is Eddie, and this is Eli."

Delphine leaned closer to the boys. "Hello, little ones. When you're a little older, you can come over and play with my grandbabies, Louisa and Lucy."

As Grace tried to weave through the clan in her brain to place them, Trahern stated, "They are the daughters of Nikki Gray-Hartley and Rafe Hartley."

Delphine nodded. "Nikki is technically my step-daughter, but she insists the girls call me Granny. But enough of my chattering. What can I help you with?"

Grace watched Trahern carefully as she answered, "Some ice cream, please. Do you have strawberry?"

"Yes, of course."

Trahern, who had been staring at the twins, glanced up at Grace. Since she couldn't read his expression, she murmured, "Did you want some?"

As her mate shifted his gaze back to the twins, her heart thudded inside her chest. She wasn't good with botany or medicine, but she was good at remembering little details about what people liked.

However, the longer he remained silent, the more Grace wondered if she'd made a mistake. Trahern liked things ordered and on a schedule, or at least as much as they could be, with the babies. This was outside of that.

Then he nodded, and she couldn't help but smile. "Brilliant. Then we'll have some ice cream, please. Although I need to see what you have so I can decide what to get."

She walked toward the back, and Trahern followed with the pram, looking pensive.

Her first instinct was to ask what he was thinking. However, he was a private person, and she didn't want to push him in public more than he could handle.

So Grace focused on the flavors in the case, adding more questions to her mental list of things to ask Trahern about later.

Even though Trahern had only mentioned liking strawberry ice cream once, Grace had remembered. More than remembered—on their first outing from the house together, she'd taken him to get some.

But why? He didn't understand.

His dragon spoke up. *She wants to know us better.*

Why? I've already vowed to protect her and the boys.

I think you need time to figure it out by yourself.

His beast fell silent, leaving him hanging. His dragon understanding things which eluded Trahern was part of the reason they'd struggled to get along from the beginning.

Which had led to his dragon all but falling silent for years, when Trahern had fled from the naked female.

His beast said softly, *We think differently. I had trouble understanding you, and vice versa. Now, I know not to push or expect you to understand what I want easily. We must work together, just as you must work with Grace, and be honest.*

Trahern lifted his gaze to watch his mate, who smiled and chatted with Delphine Gray. In just over a month, Grace had made remarkable progress, her breakdown yesterday notwithstanding. She still wouldn't tell anyone exactly what had gone on before being brought to Stonefire, beyond the bare details necessary to treat her. However, she smiled more, and sometimes laughed, which was usually a sign of improvement.

Not for the first time, he wished he could look someone in the eye and determine if it was true joy or fake. But he'd never been good at that kind of thing.

His dragon spoke up again. *I think she is happier, although I struggle to judge sometimes too.*

Before he could reply to his beast, Grace turned her smiling face at him, and his heart rate increased. He'd thought her beautiful in the sunlight, but when she smiled, he could barely string two thoughts together.

Which scared him a little.

Grace must not have noticed because she gestured toward the counter and ice cream flavors. "They have strawberry, but did you want to look and see if you want something else? And did you want a cone or a cup?"

"Strawberry in a cone is fine. It's not too hot, so it shouldn't melt over the sides. I don't like melted ice cream."

Delphine prepared their order, Trahern paid, and they each took their cones. Grace had two scoops, licked the top one, and the sight of her tongue made his skin heat.

But why?

She moaned a little, and his skin tightened more, and he started to feel overheated. His penis also filled with a little blood.

Which hadn't happened since the embarrassing incident on Snowridge. At least when awake. He awoke to uncomfortable stiffness sometimes and usually took a cold shower to douse it.

His dragon spoke up. *She is our mate. It's okay to want her. To desire her.*

Not wanting to talk about this right now, or end up with a fully erect penis in public, he turned the pram with one hand and walked toward the exit.

"Trahern, wait up!" He heard her murmured thanks to Delphine and soon caught up to him. "Where are we going? The grocery store is the other way."

After stopping, he stepped away from the pram and said, "I need a few minutes."

Without looking back, he dashed toward one of his safe places—the medicinal garden—dropping his ice cream cone, and needing a little space from anything related to Grace.

Grace, who made him feel things he thought were nuisances.

Who also confused him with her touches and licks of her tongue and pretty smiles.

Which only made more blood rush to his penis, irritating him further.

Once he entered the walled garden, he took a deep breath and started naming every plant inside his head. It would take over an hour to do them all. Maybe then he could settle his mind and push aside any sexual thoughts.

Not only because they disordered his life, but she had recently been imprisoned and given birth. To want her that way was unseemly.

So he kept reciting scientific plant names inside his head, determined to restore order to his mind and remember Grace was his mate in name only.

Grace watched Trahern stride purposefully away from her, tossing his ice cream cone to the ground in his wake, and tried to figure out what had happened.

He'd seemed pleased at her surprise and had nearly smiled when she'd handed him the cone.

But within minutes, he'd looked like a deer caught in headlights and had run away.

It shouldn't sting since he wasn't really her mate or husband or romantic partner. And yet, some of the dark weight from yesterday descended upon her shoulders, making her think she was being foolish.

"Grace?"

She distantly heard her name, but didn't fully acknowledge it. No, she was trying too hard to fight back tears. Silly tears, seeing as she'd been the one to push Trahern with her surprise.

A female dragon-shifter she didn't recognize at first, with brown hair, pale skin, and a scar on her face, appeared in front of her. Then the scar triggered her memory, from when she was newly rescued. "Dr. Turner?"

The dragonwoman's southern English accent filled her ears. "Scarlett is fine, since I'm not your doctor. What's wrong? Sid and Gregor said you were cleared of any lingering drugs and aftereffects. But you look as if a wind might push you over."

As the dragonwoman doctor searched her gaze, she remembered how the dragonwoman had been firm yet kind when Grace had first been rescued. She'd even taken some of her former fellow prisoners off for more intensive care, both medical and mental.

And yet, the thought of explaining the mess she'd made to anyone only made her more tired.

Scarlett glanced at the melting ice cream cone in her hand, then at the one on the ground a few feet away, and then at the twins. "Right, I think we need to have a chat."

"Pardon?"

Scarlett gestured toward the pram. "May I push them whilst you eat your ice cream? There's a lovely place near the lake that I like to go to when I need some peace. Even if I'm not here that often, I always like to find a hidden spot to enjoy the sound of the wind and birds and feel the sun on my face." She paused and then added, "And I think you could use a little peace."

She searched Scarlett's gray eyes, seeing only kindness and a little understanding, which confused her. The doctor didn't have any children, or a mate.

But as she heard laughter in the distance, Grace nodded. "Let's go."

The dragonwoman said nothing, merely checking that the twins were still asleep, and Grace was following. By the time they reached the small lake within Stonefire's boundaries, Grace had discarded her ice cream, and the quiet had dispelled a little of the weighty darkness.

They reached a bench placed under the trees, on the opposite side of where most people entered the lake to swim. Maybe because it was midday, few people were out and about.

Scarlett gestured toward the bench, and once Grace sat, the other woman followed suit, pulling the pram to rest between them. After a few minutes of them both staring at the water, Scarlett spoke again. "I heard you mated Dr. Trahern Lewis."

"Yes."

"Hmm." Another minute passed before Scarlett added, "My late brother was a lot like Trahern. He saw the world differently, interacted differently with his dragon, and struggled with change of any sort, more so than Dr. Lewis does."

Before she could stop herself, she echoed, "Late brother?"

As soon as she said it, Grace wished she could take it back. But rather than scold her for asking something so personal, the dragonwoman's smile turned bittersweet. "Yes. James was several years younger than me and my twin, and was one of the first to be executed under the old Skyhunter leader, once he'd determined a new pathway for his clan. Those who were 'different' or a 'drain on resources' were to be culled."

Grace frowned. She knew only a little about Clan Skyhunter—it was in the South Downs, near the coast, and had a pair of co-leaders. The clan had also suffered some sort of tragedy under the old leader, but she didn't know the details.

Still, she replied, "I'm sorry for your loss. That's horrible."

Scarlett's gaze never left the surface of the lake. "My brother was brilliant with numbers and never thought it was strange I wanted to be a doctor one day. And yes, I know there are a lot of female doctors now. However, back when I was still a kid, even before Skyhunter's ex-leader went a bit mad and started killing and imprisoning people, females were expected to mate and have children. Maybe they could be nurses or teachers. But not doctors. The job was too stressful and would harm any unborn child."

"That's rubbish. Women were working up until the day they gave birth for most of history."

"I agree. So when I was old enough, I secretly applied to a doctor training course in Scotland, was accepted, and snuck away to attend." She gripped the bench with her hands, her knuckles turning white. "Once I was gone, the ex-leader made an example and punished me and my family by killing my brother."

"Oh, Scarlett."

The dragonwoman shook her head, cleared her throat, and continued, "I went back, of course, needing to comfort my parents despite knowing what would happen to me. But the reason I'm telling you all this is because I understand how Trahern's brain works a little more than most, because of my brother. Whilst it was too painful to make it my focus of research or study, I still keep up with new developments and volunteer sometimes with dragon-shifters who struggle to communicate with others and their inner dragons." Her gaze finally met Grace's. "Trahern is a good male, and his offering to mate you means something, more than you think." Grace opened her mouth to protest, but Scarlett beat her to it. "At any rate, I want you to reach out to me anytime, with questions or frustrations or just pure curiosity. I wasn't able to help my brother, but maybe I can help you and Trahern."

As Grace studied the dragonwoman's gaze, she saw a mixture of sincerity and pain, before the latter quickly faded away.

Without thinking, she asked, "Can I give you a hug?"

Scarlett blinked. "Um, okay."

She enfolded the dragonwoman in her arms, squeezed, and released her. "Thank you."

Scarlett smiled. "I'm not sure how much help I can be, but I hope it turns out well for you and Trahern."

The dragonwoman looked like she wanted to say something else, but shook her head and stood. "I need to get back to the clinic. Are you okay to be on your own now?"

"I think so. But I want to stay and enjoy the peace and quiet whilst I can. The twins will wake up soon, and the madness will begin all over again."

Despite the words, she stared down at her twins, smiling.

"Right, well let me just give you my mobile number and then I'll be off. But reach out to me any time, I mean it. You can even, gasp, ring me."

She snorted, took out her phone, and entered Scarlett's number into her contacts. Right before she left, Scarlett murmured, "Give Trahern time, Grace. Time to adjust, time to accept new things, time to make room for you and the boys. That doesn't mean waiting forever, but rearranging his world will be a bit more jarring than it'd be for you or me. And yes, I know it's a whirlwind as a new mother. However, it will be more intense for Trahern."

With that, Scarlett waved and left Grace alone to

think of what the dragonwoman had shared and how to approach Trahern the next time she saw him.

If she saw him.

No, he would return home. He would.

She hoped.

Chapter Nine

Not wanting to go home to an empty home—Grace understood Trahern needed space, but she wanted to be around other people right now as a distraction—she headed for Dawn's house. After arriving, she knocked, and Blake opened the door, frowning. "Sorry, Grace, but it might not be the best time right now."

"What's wrong? Can I help?"

He opened his mouth to reply when Daisy appeared at his side. "Oh, Grace. Mum is crying, and I don't know why. She won't let me into the spare room, and I'm worried. I can watch the twins with my dad if you go check on her. Will you? Please?"

Grace moved her gaze to Blake, saw his flashing pupils and the grim set of his jaw, and knew something was very, very wrong. And after everything Dawn had done for her, Grace wanted to do something for her friend. "Let me help if I can, Blake. Please."

After a few seconds, he nodded curtly and motioned inside. "I'll take the boys into the living room and watch them for you. Dawn is in the spare room upstairs."

Daisy took her hand and squeezed. "Thank you, Grace. My mum sometimes thinks she can handle everything herself, but it's not always true."

The girl's cracking voice shot straight to her heart. "I'll try my best, Daisy, I promise. You and your mum are my friends, after all, and friends help each other."

Something she wouldn't have believed even a month ago.

However, as Blake herded Daisy and the pram into the living room, Grace pushed all other thoughts aside as she ascended the stairs. She heard murmured voices behind the door and hesitated before knocking. "Dawn? It's Grace."

The door opened a crack, and Dawn peered through, looking on the verge of tears. "Grace? Why are you here?"

"Daisy said you could use some help, and something is obviously wrong." As Dawn hesitated, Grace added, "Whatever it is, I can keep a secret."

The other woman bit her bottom lip and wrung her hands before nodding. "Okay. Although if you have a weak stomach, you should turn around now and go back downstairs. She's been beaten quite badly."

"Who?"

"My friend, Marianna. She's human and shouldn't be here, but I refuse to let her ex hurt her any worse. He might kill her."

A Scottish male voice she didn't recognize said, "He won't ever touch her again."

Dawn stood back, let Grace in, and closed the door.

A tall, ginger-haired man stood beside the bed, his arms crossed over his chest, and his pupils flashing. A dragonman.

Dawn rushed back to her friend's side, and Grace forced her gaze to the figure on the bed and barely contained a gasp.

The woman had black hair and light tan skin, but her face was swollen and covered in bruises, her arm was in a cast, and so was one of her legs. There were also numerous cuts on her chest and even more bruises. She looked to be unconscious.

"What happened?"

The Scottish dragonman replied, "Her ex-husband beat her, left her for dead, and kidnapped her children."

Dawn sat in a chair next to the bed and reached out to brush some hair off the woman's forehead. "Oh, Marianna. Why didn't you reach out to me? I would've helped you."

The dragonman grunted. "We can't change the past, aye? But I'm staying on Stonefire until she's well enough to be moved or we catch her bastard ex. The fewer who know she's here, the better."

Grace finally tore her gaze from Marianna and met the dragonman's. "Who are you?"

"Brodie MacNeil, from Clan Lochguard."

"Well, Brodie, I won't tell anyone, except for my mate. Trahern's a doctor and can help her."

Dawn spoke up again. "Dr. Sid has seen her, and actually has people looking for Trahern right now. She thinks one of Trahern's serums might work on her. And she desperately needs it since she had a bad reaction to dragon's blood. Apparently, Marianna is one of the few who can't have it at full strength or it might kill her."

Brodie grunted. "Aye, that's why it took us so long to get here. We had to hide for a wee while, until she was stable enough to move her."

Grace, like everyone, knew dragon's blood had healing properties. However, she'd never known some humans had a negative reaction to it. *Poor woman*, she thought.

Dawn's voice garnered her attention again. "Do you know where Trahern is?"

"No, but I can call him. He should pick up."

She hoped.

Dawn's eyes turned pleading. "Please. Her daughter and mine are good friends, and I just want Marianna to get better so we can help her."

Grace nodded, went into the hall, and dialed Trahern.

He answered on the second ring. "Grace? Are you okay?"

"I'm fine. But..." she explained what had happened, and how Dawn's friend needed his help.

He stated, "I'll head to the clinic now to retrieve supplies and rush over."

Before she could say anything else, he hung up. But relief flooded through her. Trahern had most likely saved her life during her difficult birth. If there was anyone who could help the bruised and battered woman in the other room, it was her mate.

Grace went back to comfort Dawn as they waited for Trahern, doing her best not to wither under Brodie's intense stare.

Trahern finished administering the serum to Marianna Barlow, and then briefly glanced at the dragonman from Lochguard named Brodie.

He'd refused to leave the room and had stated he was staying and would sleep on the floor.

Having dealt with stubborn dragon-shifters before, Trahern wasn't going to waste his time suggesting Brodie sleep elsewhere. So he held out a bottle of pills and stated, "Ensure she takes these to help with the pain. I'll administer another shot tomorrow and check on her. If the serum works, she should have made significant progress by then."

Brodie grunted, took the pills and went back to standing with his arms crossed, looking fierce.

Why, Trahern didn't understand. There were no enemies in the vicinity.

Rather than dwell on that, he left and headed downstairs to the kitchen, where he found Grace comforting Dawn. She kept ordering the other female to drink her tea and eat a few biscuits.

Once the human female finally ate something, Grace noticed him. Her expression met his and softened. "All done?"

"Yes. I'll be back to check on her tomorrow. And if Brodie upsets you too much, Dawn, I will ask Kai and Nikki to forcibly remove him."

Dawn shook her head. "No. Brodie's only doing his job. And..."

Grace frowned at Dawn. "And what?"

"Nothing. Thank you both for your help. I can hear your boys getting fussy, Grace. You and Trahern should go home." Grace opened her mouth to protest, but Dawn beat her to it. "I insist. I'll call you tomorrow, I promise. I have Blake and Daisy to lean on."

"If you're sure."

"I am."

Grace gave Dawn's shoulder a squeeze before standing. "If you need help, reach out to us, no matter what time it is."

Trahern added, "Yes. Inform me if her condition worsens, and I'll return quickly."

After murmuring goodbyes to Dawn, and then Blake

and Daisy, Trahern finally herded his mate and her twins out of the cottage and toward their own.

The sun had nearly set, painting the sky a mixture of orange, red, and blue. But he focused on Grace, who struggled to walk and leaned heavily on the pram. "What do you need, Grace? Tell me."

She glanced at him for a second before sighing and looking straight ahead again. "Magic, so I can take away my friend's pain, heal her friend, and stop being tired all the time?"

He frowned. "Magic doesn't exist. What people deem magic is usually an optical illusion."

Smiling, Grace glanced at him. "I was being fanciful, Trahern. Like if I asked what sort of superpower you wanted, what would it be?" He frowned deeper, and she added, "You know, like with all those superhero films? Surely you've at least heard of them?"

He adjusted his glasses. "Some of the patients talk about them. But superpowers aren't real, or even feasible, in most cases. A spider bite will not give you spider-like abilities. If anything, that amount of radiation and toxic substance would've killed the spider outright."

"Hmm, I suppose. Do you ever read fiction or watch movies just for fun and try not to dissect them?"

Trahern could brush aside the question. It would be easy enough.

And yet, he felt guilty for leaving Grace earlier, after she'd tried to surprise him with something he liked.

His dragon yawned and woke up to speak. *Stop hesi-*

tating with Grace. She will not laugh at you or look at you with pity. She is kind.

He'd had his fair share of being ridiculed over the years. *It's not that easy.*

Just try with her. Because to really help her, she needs to trust us. Only after she shares her recent past will she fully start to heal and truly be happy.

How do you know this? Happiness is subjective, not objective.

I've always understood emotions better. Won't you trust me?

For most dragon-shifters, this would be a simple question. After the first few years of speaking, they rarely doubted one another.

However, Trahern and his beast had struggled. Especially when it came to females.

His dragon spoke again. *I'm older and wiser now. I haven't pushed you about sex since the incident, have I?*

No.

All I ask is that you be honest and stop hesitating with Grace when it comes to talking. That's all.

During the chat with his beast, he'd focused straight ahead. But now, he looked back at Grace, who met his gaze again. After a beat, he blurted, "Movies and fictional stories can be confusing for me, along with TV shows. So no, I don't usually watch them unless it's an instructional video or lecture."

"Why are they confusing to you, Trahern?"

Glancing back at the cottages in the distance, he

replied, "I'm rarely able to deduce a stranger's mood or emotions. With time, I learn clues, such as body language, tone, and facial expressions, and can mentally construct a guide to decipher them. By now, I know Sid and Gregor fairly well. Same for Emily. However, small things most people would understand in a film or story fly over my head. And more often than not, it results in me not being able to follow the story." He shrugged. "So I don't watch or read fiction."

"Hmm. I never really thought about that—the small unspoken clues in films and TV. But you're right, they play an important role sometimes. However, I think you might enjoy answering silly questions with me. Shall we try?"

He wanted to brush it off. But it was getting harder and harder to tell Grace no, so he nodded.

She continued, "Right, then pretend anything is possible, putting aside science and logic, and tell me: if you could pick between being able to teleport anywhere in the world or being able to move things with the power of your thoughts alone, which would you want?"

"Neither is possible."

"No. But if they were, which would you pick?"

It was on the tip of his tongue to state neither. Because it was a waste of time to posit the impossible.

And yet, at the curiosity in Grace's eyes, he took a second to think about it. If this game made her smile, or eased her worries about Dawn for a bit, it would serve another purpose, a better one. Because he liked it when she smiled or laughed, or at least had fewer frowns.

He finally replied, "Teleportation, if possible, would be more useful."

"Useful, yes. But it also means you could travel whenever you wanted. You could enjoy sunsets in Thailand one day and then the view from Machu Picchu the next." She sighed. "That would be so lovely."

At the slight change in her tone, he asked, "You would like to travel to those places?"

She bobbed her head. "Yes, among others. I've never left the UK. And yet now, with the boys and me worrying about their biological father maybe finding us, I probably never will. I might never be able to leave Stonefire."

He could definitely detect the listlessness in her voice. Her eyes also looked a little empty to him, too.

His dragon spoke up. *She is sad and worried.*

Trahern spoke to Grace. "Stonefire is quite good at protecting humans. We have the most human mates in the entire UK."

"I know. But I overheard the guards back in the prison say..."

Her voice drifted off. Normally, Trahern would remain silent. And yet, he needed to learn of any threats to his family.

Because despite the strange circumstances of their mating, Grace, Eddie, and Eli were his family now. His to protect and take care of.

Ignoring the confusion rushing through him at where that thought had come from, he focused on Grace. "What did they say, Grace? I wish to help you, but I need the information to do so."

Her voice was soft, almost inaudible, as she stared at her sons and replied, "They said that a pair of twin dragon boys would fetch several hundred thousand pounds on the black market, and that their...*he* would get a percentage cut from the sale, since he'd turned me in originally."

At the thought of someone selling children to strangers, he clenched his fingers into fists. He did not anger easily, but hurting those who couldn't defend themselves was one of the things he detested the most.

Somehow, he needed to find a way to eradicate the threat to his family. Without thinking, which rarely happened, he stated, "I will talk to Bram and Kai."

"Trahern? Are you okay?"

He growled, actually growled, and replied, "I will ensure they find that dragonman and the DDA imprisons him. He will not hurt you or the boys, Grace. I vow it. One day you will be able to travel without worry."

Silence fell, but he couldn't look at her as he tried to pack away his anger and the urge to do harm. It hadn't happened in a long time, not since he'd come across Emily back at university, running away from a group of drunk males trying to catch her.

They had never bothered her again.

115

And yet, his anger in this moment was tenfold.

His beast spoke up. *It will not go away until you talk to Bram and Kai. Maybe not even then. But it's best to talk with them now, so they can protect our mate.*

Trahern didn't want to leave Grace again. And yet, this time it was to help her.

His beast said, *Tell her this time. So she doesn't worry.*

His cottage was about twenty feet away. "Grace, go home. I will be back later."

Her arm touched his. "Where are you going, Trahern?"

As she squeezed, a fraction of his anger eased. "I need to inform Kai and Bram to look for this bastard and tell them about the threats he poses."

"But don't they know it all already?"

"Some. But when money is involved, people go to extreme lengths to get it. It may make him desperate and reckless, which means unpredictable."

From the corner of his eye, he watched Grace's skin turn ashen. For reasons he didn't understand, he touched her cheek. "He will not hurt you or the boys, Grace. I won't let him."

Her brown eyes searched his own before nodding. "I believe you. But Trahern?"

"Yes?"

"You'll come home right after, won't you?"

"I will try." He removed his hand from her soft skin.

"Feed the boys and yourself, Grace, and then try to get some rest."

His mate hesitated a second but finally nodded and headed toward the cottage. Only after she was safely inside did he turn around and stride toward Bram's place.

Before long, he knocked at his clan leader's door. Repeatedly. Until Bram's mate, Evie, opened the door with a frown. "Trahern? What is it?"

He rarely visited the clan leader's home, preferring to talk with Sid or Gregor. However, this was too important. Grace and the boys were too important.

His dragon hummed in approval.

Trahern's pupils must've flashed, because Evie's eyes widened and she stepped aside. "Come in, then. Bram's with the children, but I'll send him to his office." She pointed down the hall. "It's down there. Will you wait?"

He nodded, thanked her, and went to the indicated room. He'd barely noted the desk, or chairs in front of it, or the bookcases full of books and binders before Bram's voice echoed behind him. "Trahern, what a surprise. If you're here, it must be important, lad. Tell me what it is."

"The threat to my mate might be bigger than we realized since he will get a lot of money if he turns in the twins. You need to find him and ensure he pays for his crimes so my mate doesn't have to worry all the time."

Bram raised his eyebrows. "Aye, well, I think we need to chat. Sit down and tell me everything you know. I can't help you if I don't have all the facts."

"But you'll look for him and ensure Grace and the boys are safe?"

"As best as I can. Now sit down, lad, and tell me everything."

Trahern didn't know Bram well, although the clan always said good things about him. Personally, Trahern had always been grateful the male had allowed him to stay on Stonefire.

So after gingerly sitting in one of the chairs, he recounted the guard's conversation and the money involved. And by the end, Bram was scowling.

Before he could ask why, Bram stated, "We've been looking for the bastard, but we'll try to make it a bigger priority now that a few other things have been taken care of. Don't worry, Trahern, we'll find him. Although if Grace could talk with Kai or even Nikki about anything else she might've remembered since returning to Stonefire, it would be helpful. Do you think she will?"

Trahern counted the binders on a shelf—eight—before answering, "I don't know, but I will ask."

"That's all I need." Bram hesitated before asking, "How are you doing with Grace?"

Emotionally exhausted from the ups and downs with his mate throughout the day, Trahern stood and replied succinctly. "Good. However, she's had a long day, is tired, and I need to return home. Please let me know once you find the bastard."

A quick glance showed the corner of Bram's mouth kicked up before he replied, "Aye, I will. Go home to your mate, Trahern. And don't hesitate to see me again if you need to. I'm always here. Goodnight, lad."

With a nod, Trahern exited the office and, thankfully, didn't run into anyone else in the hallway. Once outside, he rushed toward the clan restaurant. It was getting late, but he wanted to ensure Grace had something to eat. She'd mentioned liking pasta once. He'd get her that.

However, by the time he returned home with the food, she was sleeping on her bed, snoring slightly, and he didn't want to wake her. So he pulled the blanket up around her, did the same with each of the boys, and then retreated to his home office. The urge to wake up Grace and talk with her was strong, but he resisted.

Not only because she needed sleep, but also because Trahern knew himself. He was already getting attached to Grace and if he gave in to the urge once, he'd want to make it a part of his routine.

However, Grace wasn't really his mate. His friend, maybe. But that was all. He had no right to demand so much of her time. Especially since once he adjusted his routine to include her, it would be difficult to stop.

So, he would be careful and look after her, protect her, and be her friend, but nothing more. It had to be that way, to save both of their sanities.

Even if his stomach swirled and his dragon huffed, neither liking the distance.

Chapter Ten

Over the next few weeks, Grace and Trahern settled into a routine.

Whenever Trahern was home, he helped out with the twins, ensured she had enough to eat or took a nap to rest, and was always courteous to her.

And yet, whenever Grace tried to ask silly questions or convince Trahern to watch a movie with her, he always found a way to be nice enough but decline. He explained that he needed to follow as much of his normal routine as possible or his mind wouldn't settle, and then he wouldn't be able to focus on his work.

Since she'd read a few of the articles Dr. Scarlett Turner had sent her about others like Trahern, she knew he wasn't making it up—he truly needed structure. While Trahern could adapt more easily than some, he couldn't just rearrange his life because he'd mated Grace in name only.

So she'd done her best to let Trahern keep as much of his former life as possible, even if she yearned to have more days like the one with the ice cream and the walk home.

The only good thing was that Dawn's friend had mostly healed—physically—and was still secretly staying on Stonefire. Marianna didn't say a lot, but she'd allowed Dawn to share more with Grace about her ex and her children and how loads of dragon Protectors, from various clans, were still trying to track them down.

Marianna's circumstances had also made Grace realize she had a lot of things to be thankful for, even when factoring in her ex and the prison.

Despite all his faults, she couldn't imagine Trahern ever hurting her deliberately.

Although she still had nightmares every once in a while, she'd been able to hide them from Trahern. Once, when she'd woken up screaming, she'd lied to him, and it still made her uneasy, given her promise to be honest.

However, she didn't want to burden him with her past. Instead, she'd merely said she'd remembered the pain of childbirth, when she'd nearly died.

And the bloody nice dragonman had ensured Dawn came over with biscuits before leaving for work.

Between her growing friendships with the humans on Stonefire, plus her boys being healthy and showing more of their personalities every day, she should be happy. Or at least content.

And yet, as she watched Trahern make her breakfast like he always did, loneliness washed over her. She had no right to ask more of him, and yet she missed how he used to talk with her every morning about the clan or his work or, on rare occasions, about his past.

That had stopped abruptly the day after the ice cream incident.

Every day she wanted to scream, "Why?"

And yet, she'd held back, always smiling at him before he left for work.

This morning, however, she was tired after a rough night with the boys—they'd fussed and she'd barely slept at all—and her restraint faded. Once he set the plate of eggs and toast in front of her, she reached out and took his hand.

Trahern froze, staring down at where her fingers wrapped around his. Before he could bolt, she whispered, "Why did you pull away and stop talking with me in the mornings?"

He frowned, but avoided her gaze.

She persisted, though, too exhausted to worry about making him uncomfortable. "Did I do something to upset you? Or did I say something wrong? I've tried to figure it out, but I can't think of anything. Especially since you said you weren't upset about the ice cream surprise, all those weeks ago."

For a few beats, he remained silent. Despite how silly and ridiculous it was, her eyes heated with tears.

No doubt, he was trying to think of a way to be polite and not hurt her feelings.

Releasing him, she murmured, "Don't worry about it. You'll be late for work. You should go."

"Grace."

At the tortured sound of his voice, she glanced up and noticed his flashing dragon eyes. The pupils changed between round and slitted, faster than she'd ever seen before.

What was his dragon saying?

She must've spoken out loud because Trahern closed his eyes and put his head in his hands. "I can't."

"Can't what, Trahern?"

His fingers threaded through his hair, and he remained silent. Grace was torn between reaching out to comfort him and crying out in frustration.

With a groan, he said, "You."

Grace stiffened. "What about me?"

He shook his head. "I can't. Not fair."

And then it all made sense—he felt trapped, but didn't want to hurt her by telling her so.

It shouldn't sting, and yet her throat tightened.

Not wanting to break down and make Trahern uncomfortable, she stood and turned to flee. However, before she could, Trahern's hand gripped her wrist gently. "Grace."

"Let me go, Trahern. Please."

"No. Not until you understand."

She swallowed. "I understand. I'll talk to Bram and see what can be done."

Confusion tinged his voice. "About what?"

"About freeing you from the burdens you don't want."

With a growl, he tugged and turned her to face him.

At the flashing eyes, filled with something dangerous, her voice died in her throat.

He quickly stated, "What I want is not good for you, Grace."

Frowning, she blurted, "What are you talking about?"

He stepped closer, to the point she could feel the heat of his body. His grip gentled before he strummed his thumb against her inner wrist. Back and forth, slowly, making her skin heat and her heart pound.

And she waited, hoping for the impossible but trying her best to tamp down her expectations.

Trahern had tried to enforce distance and walls, he really had.

No matter how much harder it'd become to leave her each day, he'd tried to protect Grace. From him. From his possible obsession.

From his dragon's yearnings and cravings.

It had seemed the only rational option, to spend as

little time as possible with her. And yet, this morning, when she'd thought he didn't want her as his mate, something had snapped.

And now his dragon growled and paced as he said, *Don't you bloody dare let her leave us. She's ours. Stop fighting it. Stop fighting me.*

Over the past weeks, he'd managed to convince his beast to drop the matter. To let him focus on work and research and anything but Grace and the boys.

It'd grown a little harder each day, but Trahern had remained in control.

Now, however, he sensed his dragon's uneasiness, as if he might snap and go rogue.

He said to his beast, *Don't do this.*

She is our mate. Whilst I can wait to claim her completely, I need her. She must remain ours. Don't push her away again.

What can I do? I'm not like other people. If I allow her too close and she decides to leave, I will not survive it.

His dragon's voice gentled a little, but was still gruff as he said, *If you don't let her in and push her away, I won't survive it.*

Trahern's dragon had never been dramatic or said things he didn't mean, which made the words all the more serious.

Despite their fractious relationship over the years, Trahern had taken secret comfort in the second presence inside his head. Even if they hadn't spoken much since the incident years ago, it'd helped him feel a little less alone.

He couldn't fail his beast.

And yet, he didn't want to hurt Grace, either.

His dragon spoke up again. *You won't. I've noticed how she looks at us with longing, and even rare glimpses of desire. She is already our mate by law. Why won't you try to woo her in truth?*

Trahern's brain focused on the desire part of his dragon's words.

Normally, the thought of his skin touching another's, being dirtied by sweat and other bodily fluids, made him shudder and want to take a shower.

However, as Grace stared up at him with her dark brown eyes, her pulse beating under his thumb on her inner wrist, all he could think about was getting closer to her. Feeling more of her skin. Breathing in her scent. His eyes dropped to her mouth, wondering what she tasted like.

Alarm bells sounded in his head, but Grace's voice snapped him back to the present. "Trahern? Are you all right?"

His gaze met hers again. Her eyes were beautiful, framed by dark lashes and full of concern—one of the emotions he'd learned about her—for him.

A rush of wanting coursed through Trahern, and his voice sounded husky to his own ears as he said, "Do you want the truth, even if it makes you uncomfortable?"

Frowning, she nodded. "The truth, always. Brutally honest is what you mentioned, right?"

Unable to resist, he raised his free hand and traced her cheek. Grace's lips parted a fraction, and she sucked in a breath. Her pupils dilated, most likely from desire and lust. He didn't think she was afraid of him.

"I stayed away to protect you, Grace. Because if I let myself spend time with you, talk with you, get to know you, then I would want to talk with you every day. To make you part of my routine. One that I would struggle to break or recover from."

She searched his gaze. "I don't understand."

He continued tracing her cheek, her jaw, and even her lips. "You are beautiful, Grace." He traced her bottom lip and then the top one. "I've never been drawn to another female before. To want and even touch her. And then you showed up, confusing me."

"Confused you how?"

He studied her lips instead of her eyes, needing a second to gather his courage.

His dragon spoke up. *Just tell her.*

Returning his eyes to hers, he replied, "I want to be your mate in truth, Grace. But doing that means you may not like how much I will focus on you, how much and often I'll want you."

Her gaze softened, and she gingerly placed a hand on his chest. Her touch sent a rush of warmth through him, easing both man and beast a little.

He was still terrified that she'd reject him. However, he did his best to be patient and wait for her answer.

She murmured, "I want to try, but..." He waited, and she eventually continued, "I need to know you won't pull or run away again. If you need a break, then tell me. If you need some time alone, tell me. But closing yourself off and shutting me out hurts, Trahern. It'll be even worse if I finally share more of myself, only to have you reject me again."

He wanted to proclaim he'd never do that, never shut her out, would be more normal for her, and everything would work out perfectly.

But Trahern was far from perfect. It would take work to do as she asked, to not close off and protect himself. And even then, he'd probably still fail sometimes.

His beast spoke up again. *It will be difficult, but the prize is worth it.*

Searching Grace's eyes, he replied, *She is worth it.*

Then kiss her. No, it won't start the frenzy. I'm stronger than other dragons, somewhat more independent out of necessity. A taste will be enough.

Maybe he should ask his dragon more about being independent out of necessity. And yet, all he could do was stare at Grace's lips and ache to feel her skin against his, to learn her taste, and ease some of the sadness in her eyes over the last few weeks.

Sadness probably caused by him.

But first, he needed to make a vow. Maybe the most

important one of his life. "I vow to be honest and open with you, Grace. I will not reject you. Whilst I'm not perfect, and will probably make many mistakes, know this—I want you. Always. Will you be my mate in truth?"

Her other hand lifted and cupped his cheek. As her fingers stroked his skin, he leaned into her touch, and his beast hummed.

"Yes, Trahern. I will be your mate in truth. But just know I'm not perfect, either. And we'll probably argue or disagree or maybe even shout at each other sometimes, and that's normal. As long as we talk and don't keep our feelings secret, we'll be okay in the end."

He frowned. "I'll try. But this is new to me. All of it."

She smiled. "I know."

He blurted, "May I kiss you?"

Her eyebrows shot up. "Y-you want to kiss me?"

"I can wait, if you want. I won't rush you. Especially since it will be my first time, and I won't know what I'm doing."

Her lips kicked up into another smile. "I want to kiss you, too. But I have to know—will it start a frenzy? I'm not ready for that, no matter how much I want to feel your lips against me."

He shook his head. "My dragon thinks you are our true mate but assures me there won't be a frenzy."

"How is that possible?"

He rubbed one of her curls between his fingers, wanting to lift it to his nose to breathe her in.

However, his dragon grunted. *Answer her.*

With effort, he moved his gaze from her hair to her eyes again. "I am a dragon-shifter, and yet, I'm different. My dragon and I are not as close as some, and it takes greater effort to work together to even shift. There is little research on the interplay between the human and dragon halves in those like me, but I've done what I can. The link is not as strong, and as a result, there might never be a mate-claim frenzy at all."

The fingers on his chest stroked slowly, making his body heat and blood rush to his penis. However, he focused on her soft lips as she replied, "Might being the operative word."

"Then I will give you something to counteract it, if my dragon does end up demanding a frenzy."

He rushed out of the room, into his study, and went to his locked medical cabinet on the wall. After unlocking it, he found what he needed and rushed back to the kitchen. He offered the vial and syringe. "This will make my inner dragon silent for a few days. If my pupils remain slitted and he takes control to claim you, then inject me with this. I will even pre-fill the syringe for you."

As she studied him, he did exactly that and held it out to her. After a beat, she took it and laid it on the table.

He frowned. "It would be more efficient to keep it in your hand."

She touched his face again, making his dragon hum.

"Perhaps. But I don't want the memory of your first kiss to be one of me holding a syringe."

Glancing at the table, he stated, "I don't want to hurt you or make you do something you don't want to do, though."

Her thumb rubbed against his chin. "I know. And the lengths you've gone to show me is enough. Now, kiss me, Trahern. Please."

After closing his eyes and lowering his head, he gently pressed his lips to Grace's and retreated. The touch had been nice and warm. Although he didn't understand the constant need to kiss, like so many others he knew who snuck off to do it often with their mates.

"Trahern?"

"Hmm?"

"My turn."

She pulled his head down again and started the same, with pressing her lips to his. But then she focused on taking his bottom one between hers, then the top, and kept doing it. He followed her lead as he stroked the side of her neck, feeling her quickening pulse under his fingers, his skin heating and his penis growing harder.

Then she seamed his lips with her tongue, and he opened on instinct. As soon as her tongue entered his mouth, he wanted more. More of her heat. More of her taste. More of her skin.

Stroking his tongue against hers, he groaned. With each second, he took more control, until he chased her tongue into her mouth, exploring, possessing, wanting more of her.

His hands wandered to her lovely arse, gripped, and pulled her against his arousal. She moaned, sending shivers through his body, to the tip of his cock.

He continued tasting his female, learning what she liked, and reveling in her scent and heat and taste.

Eventually, her fingers stroked his jaw, and she slowed her tongue, until she finally pulled away. Trahern moved to follow her, but she pressed a finger over his lips as she breathed heavily.

He could smell her arousal and knew she'd liked it. Why would she stop?

Grace's voice cut through his raging need for her. "We need to take a break."

He growled. "Why? You enjoyed it. So did I. Let's kiss some more."

She never removed her finger. "Can't you hear them? The boys are crying."

His heart had beat so hard, her taste and scent had consumed his every sense, that he'd ignored the rest of the world.

However, as he listened, he finally heard the faint cries from the twins.

Stepping away, he shook his head. "I'm sorry. I warned you about my intensity and focus."

She followed him and took his hand. "Don't apologize. You've never done any of this before, have you?"

Gazing off to the side, he murmured, "No."

"Then of course it's going to be intense, which isn't a bad thing." He continued to stare off to the side, his heart thudding, and she stated, "Look at me, Trahern."

He did, and she replied, "You want honesty? Well, here it is—I didn't want to stop kissing you, either."

"You didn't?"

She squeezed his fingers in hers. "No. I like your intensity, your focus and enthusiasm. It makes me feel like the only woman in the world."

"You are the only female in the world to me, in a sexual way."

"Oh, Trahern." She removed her finger and barely brushed her lips against his before releasing him. "We'll kiss more later. You need to go to work, and I need to check on the twins."

He hesitated, not wanting to leave her. Or the boys.

He wanted to stay.

She smiled. "I'll be waiting for later, once we're alone. Use that as motivation."

With that, Grace walked out of the kitchen, swaying her hips, and he couldn't move until she was gone.

His dragon finally spoke up. *Soon, you must share her with me.*

Not yet, dragon.

She is fully healed, thanks to shots of our dragon's blood. But you're not quite ready, are you?

Considering he was already thinking of kissing Grace again, maybe for hours, he could only imagine how much more he'd be distracted if sex was as enjoyable as everyone made it out to be. He replied, *No, not yet.*

Then, I will be patient a little while longer. Just don't push her away.

I'm going to try not to, dragon. I promise.

As his beast grunted and fell silent, Trahern hurried to clean up the kitchen and head to the clinic. Today was his rotation to see urgent cases, and he couldn't brush it off.

But unlike most days, he didn't mind seeing lots of people, touching them briefly, or filling out the paperwork. Each person helped pass the time until he could finally see Grace again.

She was his now, and he was determined to remind her of that as much as possible.

Chapter Eleven

It took nearly two weeks of kissing Trahern whenever they were alone before he finally agreed to go on a picnic with her and the twins.

Although as she finished packing the nappy bag for the day, her mind drifted back to his earlier kiss, one that had ended with her nearly humping his leg.

He'd become obsessed with making her hotter, teasing her with lips and tongue and teeth, and making her constantly yearn for more.

And he'd only kissed her mouth, and from her neckline up to her hair.

She hadn't even removed her shirt yet, for crying out loud.

Still, she'd never felt like this before. Almost as if he really did think she was the most beautiful woman in the world. One he treasured and devoured and craved.

The little voice inside her head warned that she'd been charmed before. However, she quickly tamped it back down. Trahern had done more for her than that bastard ever had, many times over. She wouldn't compare the two.

Not wanting to dwell on her past, Grace glanced at her boys in the pram and rearranged the little hats on their heads. "You're both getting so big already. At this rate, we're going to have to get you some new clothes again in a week or two."

Eli bashed the little stuffed dragon toy in his hand against the side of the pram, babbling like he always did. Eddie merely held his little toy and watched everyone with wide eyes.

She'd worried at first about Eddie being fussy yet quiet, but Trahern, Sid, and Gregor had all assured her the boys seemed to be fine and didn't suffer any aftereffects from the drugs she'd been given. Some babies were just quieter and more reserved than others.

Trahern emerged with the little wagon full of supplies for their picnic, and Grace smiled at him. "We don't need that much stuff. We're only going out for a few hours."

He readjusted his glasses. "I want to be prepared. The weather may turn cold or rainy at any moment."

"Well, then let's hurry to this secret spot of yours before the sun goes away."

He nodded, stared at her lips, shook his head, and started pulling the wagon. "This way."

Grace pushed the pram, and after a few seconds of companionable silence, she glanced at Trahern. As the sun reflected off his lenses, she asked, "Why do you wear glasses? I thought dragon-shifters didn't need them."

"Most don't. I caught a rare disease as a child. It went untreated for too long, and my sight deteriorated in my left eye."

"I'm so sorry." She hesitated, but reminded herself to be blunt with Trahern. "Your father didn't take you to a doctor as soon as you were ill?"

"No. I was sick for three days before he even noticed. I always wondered if he'd found a way to infect me deliberately, hoping I'd die."

"Trahern, that's horrible."

"Yes. But it was far from his first attempt to kill me in a way that made it look natural. But I was clever and learned to watch out for him as I aged. I knew more about plants than he did, so he could never poison me, even though he tried."

Unable to help herself, Grace took his empty hand in hers and squeezed. After stiffening a second, Trahern squeezed her back before threading their fingers together.

As much as she enjoyed kissing, happiness washed over her as she held Trahern's hand. His solid presence was coming to mean so much to her already.

Eli started babbling again and nearly tossed his dragon out of the pram. Grace caught it, tucked it back beside her son, and softly told him not to throw his toys.

She half-listened as Trahern went into detail about trajectories and how one day, he'd teach Eli how to best utilize his height and strength to throw greater distances.

Grace studied Trahern as he talked. He'd gone through so much, and it couldn't have been easy to share his past with her.

And what had she done to repay that trust? Not much—she'd barely revealed anything to him.

She knew it was unfair. And yet, she was afraid to open that box and see what happened.

However, more and more she yearned for a life as Trahern Lewis's mate in truth. And unless she started telling him about some of her painful memories, there wouldn't be any real future for them.

Before she could talk herself out of it, in the next lull she said softly, "I spent six months inside that prison."

He glanced at her, but she kept her gaze on her sons. They kept her grounded and were the reason she'd pushed aside the difficult memories to carry on as normally as she could.

For them, she also needed to be brave about her time inside. She wouldn't fully heal until she did.

And out of everyone, she trusted Trahern the most.

After taking a deep breath, she continued, "I don't remember most of it, though. I was drugged and kept in a room with an attached toilet. I spent most of my time staring out the window, finding shapes in the clouds. Or, memorized who came and went, just in case I found a chance to escape.

"However, as my pregnancy progressed, and I grew bigger and bigger, I knew I'd never be able to run or climb or get away." Reaching out an arm, she traced Eli's cheek and then Eddie's. "These two kicked a lot, helping to distract me. But as the months went by, I started to wonder if the prison staff would ever let me hold them. The drugs made my thoughts hazy, and yet I'd slowly pieced together how they intended to take my boys, raise them as loyal soldiers in their fight, and test out some new equipment on them. I never learned what type exactly, but even the little I overheard terrified me, to the point I started to think death might be our only way to escape."

She lifted her gaze to the hills in the distance. She hadn't meant to mention the last part, she really hadn't. So much for keeping this lighter for their picnic.

Trahern squeezed her hand and stated, "But you're here now, Grace. You and Eddie and Eli."

She looked at her sons and smiled. "We are." Her eyes moved to Trahern's. "When I thought I was going to die in childbirth, all I wanted to do was live. To be with my sons and love them the way I'd always wanted to be loved as a child. And you made that happen with your magical serum, Trahern. Thank you."

His pupils flashed a second before he cleared his throat and looked away. "I don't know if it saved you for certain. It needs to be tested more to determine its efficacy."

Grace could force herself to share more about the

bastard who tricked her and handed her over to the prison. Share the heartbreak and sense of betrayal and his eyes changing into those of a monster.

But as the sun broke from the clouds and light danced upon a small lake in the distance, she decided it could wait. She wanted to have a nice, fun day with her mate and her boys.

So, she changed the subject. "Tell me about your research with children and inner dragons. When will you get to see little Freya again?"

And as she listened, Trahern's voice helped chase away the past and some of the shadows. Even just sharing a little had made her feel lighter already.

Trahern had never experienced a surge of rage or the need to hurt others before, until Grace had said she'd been so depressed and terrified of what might happen to her children that she'd thought about ending it all.

He knew there was more she wasn't telling him. While Trahern didn't know all of Grace's history, he'd assisted Dr. Sid and Dr. Turner with some of the former prisoners. Hayley Beckett had also recounted what she'd seen.

And since Trahern wasn't a Protector or any kind of warrior, he had focused his talents on counter-serums, antidotes, and even ways of incapacitating large numbers of humans without killing them or hurting dragon-shifters.

Bloody dragon hunters. He looked forward to the day they lost most of their power and dragon-shifters had more equal footing.

For now, however, he answered Grace's questions about his work, sensing she wanted to change the subject. He'd become a lot better at reading her expressions and moods, although he still wasn't an expert.

His dragon had helped him navigate it all, too. While working more and more together was tiring, he was learning to appreciate his beast's input, especially when it came to Grace and the twins.

His family.

Even if he hadn't claimed Grace, or worked up the courage to try, he enjoyed kissing her. And holding her hand. A lot. Both things he never thought he'd like, let alone crave.

But he had a different goal today, one he was nervous about. So much so, his palms sweated more and more the closer they got to the lake.

Because he wanted to show Grace and the boys his dragon form.

His beast spoke up. *We'll work together and shift easier this time, you'll see.*

Doing so in the past had always taken work and time. True, Trahern's dragon had never spoken to him as much as he had over the last two months, so maybe it would be easier.

His dragon spoke again. *Don't fight me as I take control. If you don't, then shifting will go a lot smoother.*

Trahern had never liked handing over control to his beast. Most dragon-shifters didn't hesitate. And yet, the one time his dragon had tried to contain him in order to claim the naked female all those years ago still made him reluctant.

His dragon stated, *I won't try to claim Grace, no matter how much I want to. She isn't ready, nor are you. I just want her and our sons to see our dragon form.*

It was the first time his beast had referred to Eli and Eddie as theirs, and a sense of rightness settled over Trahern. He may not be their biological father, but they would need a lot of guidance on being dragon-shifters as they grew up. Guidance on topics he still needed to master himself.

As he glanced at Grace making silly faces at the twins, he smiled. Yes, for her and the boys, he could do this and become proficient at it. He replied, *We'll show her today. No matter how long it takes.*

His beast sniffed. *It will be faster than before. Trust me.*

He did. Mostly.

They reached the willow tree near the lake, and he gestured toward it. "Here's a well-placed spot with some sun, but we can also easily move under the willow branches for shade, if needed. There is also a large area next to it for my surprise."

Grace's gaze moved to his. Unlike with most other people, he didn't feel the urge to look away.

She raised her eyebrows. "Surprise? What kind of surprise?"

"One you'll like, I think. Let's set everything up, ensure the boys are dry and fed, and I'll show you."

He quickly unpacked the blanket and little supportive pillows for the boys, and lifted Eli out of the pram since Eddie had shown a recent preference for Grace.

Once he placed Eli in his supportive pillow and Grace did the same for Eddie, he retreated from the blanket and cleared his throat. "Do you want me to show you my surprise?"

As she settled between the twins, she nodded. "Of course. You always seem to know exactly what I want, Trahern. It's lovely."

At her soft tone and gaze, his heart warmed a little. Only because he'd learned to tame his desire a little over the past weeks did he not get an erection.

His dragon snorted. *Eventually, it will be useful.*

Ignoring his beast, he replied to Grace, "I want to show you my dragon."

"Really, Trahern?" Her tone had risen a little, meaning she was probably excited.

"Yes." He debated ending it there, but remembered his vow of honesty. "I've been working on shifting with my dragon. It's not as difficult as before."

She beamed at him, making his heart skip a beat. "Then show us, Trahern. Eddie and Eli have never seen someone shift, and I'm glad the first one is you."

Removing his glasses, he held them out, and Grace took them. The vision in his right eye was perfect, but his left one was blurry. Together, they blurred everything a little.

Still, this was one of the places he'd used to practice shifting with his dragon, so he moved confidently, to about ten feet away. With his back to Grace, he stated, "I must take off my clothes. You can close your eyes, and I'll let you know when I'm done."

"No. I want to watch you."

Her words sent a rush of heat through his body, which confounded him. Dragon-shifters, and especially doctors, didn't view nudity as anything special. But apparently, imagining Grace's eyes on him made it much harder to keep his penis from reacting.

Doing his best to recite complex formulas in his head, Trahern removed his clothing—folding it into a pile as he went—and then turned toward Grace. He couldn't make out her features without his glasses, until he closed his left eye.

Her gaze traveled his body, focusing on his genitals. Before she reacted either positively or negatively, he closed his remaining eye and spoke to his dragon. *I'm ready.*

It'd taken a lot of practice, but Trahern allowed his dragon to the forefront of his mind as he retreated to the back. Within seconds, he could feel his nose elongating to a snout, wings growing from his back, and his arms and legs morphing into limbs, and his nails into talons, until he was fully shifted.

His dragon opened its eyes, zeroed in on Grace, and waited to see how she reacted.

Grace had been told repeatedly that dragon-shifters didn't view nudity as strange or unusual and was just a part of life. She'd tried to adopt that mindset as Trahern undressed, but as he removed his trousers and revealed a firm arse, heat flooded her body.

Even watching him fold his clothing made her smile. But once he faced her, revealing his front, her mouth went dry and every other thought left her head.

He wasn't as heavily muscled as some of the dragonmen—he was leaner. And yet, his solid chest covered with a sprinkling of dark hair, along with his firm arms and broad shoulders, made her skin even warmer. She should've stopped there, but hadn't been able to resist darting a glance at his cock. While mostly flaccid, it was long and thick, and she could only imagine what it'd feel to have that inside of her.

After all, Trahern was thorough with everything. He was bound to be with sex as well.

What are you doing? Stop it. Trahern barely tolerated kissing and touching. His one near-sexual experience, from what she'd gathered, had been terrifying and embarrassing.

He might not wish to go all the way, although Grace rather hoped he would someday.

Thankfully, his body glowed faintly and started to change shape, distracting her, and she gasped as he morphed and grew, until he was a tall, majestic green dragon.

He slowly opened his wings behind him, the sunlight shining through them slightly, and her jaw dropped. The green beast looked like something from a fantasy painting or book cover.

Then the dragon tilted his head and blinked at her, and she found her voice. "Eli, Eddie, look at Trahern's dragon form. Isn't he bloody amazing?"

Both of her boys stared at the dragon, and she wished she could lift them both at the same time to give them a closer look.

However, before showing either of her boys, Grace wanted to touch Trahern's scales. Maybe scratch behind the ear, as Dawn and the others had told her to do.

After ensuring the twins were secure and wouldn't be able to roll or wiggle out of their supportive pillows, she stood and walked toward Trahern. His dragon lowered his head just as she reached him, and Grace extended a hand. "I want to pet you. Can I?"

The dragon nodded, and she ran her fingers over his snout. Green scales glinted in the sun, and were warm and smooth, like polished leather. The dragon started to hum, and she smiled. "If you like that, then you should like this better, I think." She moved until she could see the dragon's ear. "Lower your head a little more, please."

The dragon complied, and Grace found the little patch of skin behind the ear where there weren't any scales. She scratched her nails lightly, and the dragon's humming increased. Glancing over her shoulder, she saw her boys were still watching with big eyes.

Even though she wanted more time to explore Trahern's dragon form, she couldn't hog him all to herself. So she said, "I'm going to bring Eddie and Eli over one at a time. They should see you up close, too."

The dragon nodded, and she reluctantly removed her hand but not before giving the snout a quick pat and smiling at the single dragon eye she could see.

After trying to read his expression and failing, Grace finally turned and went to fetch Eddie first, who was the most animated she'd seen to date.

Having Grace's fingers scratch behind Trahern's ear had been pure bliss, for both man and beast.

His dragon hummed as they watched her pick up Eddie. *I want her to pet me again. We need to shift more often for our mate.*

Before Grace, Trahern never would've desired changing forms often. It'd always been a battle, one he'd been afraid to lose, and had worried he might turn rogue.

However, the earlier fears and nervousness had faded significantly. His dragon was happy, and Trahern nearly trusted him.

His beast said softly, *You will trust me soon. I was young before, and impatient.*

And I was damaged and afraid.

Together, we fucked up badly.

Yes, but Grace and the boys have forced us to work together. And I'm...glad.

Me, too.

For the first time in his life, Trahern appreciated the second personality inside his head. He and his dragon almost felt like...friends.

His beast grunted. *We* are *friends.*

Trahern wanted to believe his beast, to trust him completely.

But he wasn't quite there yet.

However, before he could think of how to reply, Grace stood in front of them again, with Eddie in her arms. The little boy stared up with big eyes and reached a hand toward his face.

His dragon lowered his head until the boy could lightly slap his hand against their snout.

Grace said, "Be gentle, Eddie. Don't hit the dragon. Pet him. Like this."

As his female's fingers stroked his snout again, both man and beast hummed.

The sound didn't frighten the female or the boy.

Instead, Eddie started to babble as his mother helped him pet his dragon's snout.

Something shifted in Trahern's heart at the sight. He'd worried about not being able to help the twins as they grew up. Worried that he couldn't help them with understanding inner dragons. Or be able to teach them how to defend themselves against bullies.

And yet, as the little hand stroked his scales, Trahern knew he'd do whatever it took to protect Eddie and Eli.

And Grace.

No matter what Trahern had to face or overcome, he'd do it for them. They needed him, and he would step up.

His dragon spoke up. *Of course we will. I have faith in you.*

The words made Trahern a little more hopeful about the future he wanted.

One where he could kiss and claim his mate whenever he wished.

One where Eddie and Eli might even have a sibling.

One where Trahern would be the opposite of his father and treasure the precious boys instead of trying to change them with pain and fear.

Grace kissed his snout and whispered, "Let me get Eli now. Then you can shift back, and I'll kiss you for real."

He watched his mate as she retrieved their other son. As she bent over, need rushed through him.

He wanted to see her naked, too. And he wanted to try and do more than kiss her mouth.

Some of the taunts from his younger days, right after he'd been humiliated with that female, tried to rush forth. However, he pushed them back.

Grace was different. Hell, he was different.

And he was determined to lose his virginity soon. Very soon.

Chapter Twelve

Ever since Trahern had shifted back to his human form, Grace struggled to concentrate.

The blasted man had never put his shirt back on.

With most men, she'd think it was because he was either hot or wanted to seduce her.

However, with Trahern, she didn't know what to expect.

They'd both focused on playing with the twins until they'd fallen asleep. Once she'd moved them to the pram and extended the top over her boys to shade them, as well as made sure they were buckled in, she stood staring for a second to gather her thoughts. How honest could she be with Trahern about wanting more than a kiss? The last thing she wanted was to scare him.

And yet, never being truthful meant never getting what she wanted.

Then he stood behind her, his heat warming her back, and his hands went to her waist. As his thumbs stroked her sides, her heart raced and her breathing quickened.

She tried to turn around, but Trahern kept her in place as he nuzzled her neck. "Grace."

His husky voice rolled over her, and she shivered. "Yes?"

"You're my mate."

As he nipped her neck where it met her shoulder, she managed to moan. "Yes."

"I very much enjoy kissing you."

His hand moved around to her belly, and stroked it slowly, back and forth. Her brain turned to mush, and she murmured, "Mmm."

"I would like to kiss you more. Everywhere. With no clothes on."

Heat flushed her body at the image of Trahern's head between her thighs.

Maybe she should ask and ensure he was ready for such a big step.

And yet, as he continued to stroke her belly and nuzzle her neck, she didn't want to break the moment. If he said no at any point, she'd back off.

But for now, she only wanted to encourage him. "Yes, please. I want that too."

Slowly, his hand moved from her belly up to her breast. He cupped her, and she sucked in a breath as he lightly ran a finger over her nipple.

Then his hand moved further south, until he cupped between her thighs and rocked the heel of his hand against her. She arched into his touch as she moaned again.

"Come with me, Grace. We'll go under the willow tree, and I can kiss you some more. The twins are close enough we can hear them if they wake up, but we can still have a little privacy."

She nodded, and Trahern removed his hand. Grace wanted to drag it back, but resisted and allowed him to guide her.

As they walked, she drank in his chest and focused on the tattoo on his upper arm. She traced the design with a finger and loved how her dragonman shivered and groaned at her touch.

Once under the branches of the willow tree, she'd barely noticed the blanket on the ground before Trahern unbuttoned her jeans.

She blinked, but let him undo them and tug them down. She helped wiggle out of them, and then he tugged off her shirt.

As his finger traced her collarbone, between her breasts, over her bra, her clit throbbed and wetness rushed between her legs.

With barely-there touches, Trahern Lewis had made her more aroused than she'd ever been in her life.

Then he trailed his finger to her stomach and stopped where her stretch marks were the worst and stated, "I'm glad you survived, Grace. Both your past and the birth."

He continued to stroke the marks, back and forth, and a rush of tenderness warmed her heart. "So am I."

His heated gaze met hers, his pupils flashing a few times before he said, "I won't claim you completely yet. But I want to kiss your entire body. Memorize every inch. Ensure I don't leave any part untouched or explored. Will you let me?"

She brushed a lock of hair off his forehead and then cupped his jaw. As she ran her thumb back and forth, he leaned into her touch. "Yes, I want your mouth on me very much."

It wasn't the sexiest or most romantic way to say things, but this was Trahern. And with her dragonman, she would always be honest. Innuendoes or dirty talk wasn't for him.

His gaze heated further, and he ran a hand under the band of her underwear. "Take these off. Please."

She did, and then stood only in her bra. He traced the edge of the big cup, needed because she was still nursing. "I will kiss these later. When you're not so sore."

Maybe it should be embarrassing that he knew how difficult it'd been for her to feed her two dragon boys enough, but oddly it wasn't. This was Trahern. He simply wanted facts and acted accordingly. He wouldn't mock her for the truth.

She took his free hand and guided it between her thighs. "Touch me here. Please."

As he lightly ran a finger through her center, he growled and took her mouth in a fierce kiss. He lapped and stroked, all while teasing her clit and her core, making her pant and squirm and need more. So much more. "Trahern. Stop teasing me with light touches."

His gaze burned before looking down at where he was caressing her. Watching as his fingers teased her made her even hotter, especially as he determined the pressure and pace she liked.

As she braced a hand on his shoulder to remain upright, her gaze traveled over his muscled chest, down to his straining cock behind his trousers. Yearning shot through her, wanting to drive him as wild as he made her.

But then his words garnered her attention before she could do anything. "I've researched what to do, but have never tried it before. Let me see if I can make you orgasm, Grace." His eyes met hers again. "With my mouth."

Her knees nearly buckled. "Yes. Please, yes."

His lips twitched a second before he helped Grace lay down on her back, his body settling between her thighs until his face was a few inches from hers. As he stroked his knuckles down her cheek, he murmured, "My mate."

She nodded, and he kissed her. First, he lingered on

her mouth, making her squirm and hot and desire more. So much more.

Then he went to work, his mouth exploring everywhere, from her forehead to her neck and down her torso.

And after he pushed her legs wider, he stared at her core and stroked a finger through her center. She swore she heard him growl, "Mine to claim."

But before she could think too much on his words, Trahern took her mouth in a fierce kiss again, and everything but the feel of Trahern's lips and tongue and fingers left her mind.

Trahern's penis throbbed and ached, and he was tempted to try claiming his mate fully.

But once he'd kissed his way down her body and was level with her vagina, her scent made his mouth water.

He wanted this.

His dragon spoke up. *Then tease and lap and stroke her pussy.*

His beast's words sent more blood to his penis. How he wanted her.

Then kiss her, his dragon stated. *No matter what, Grace will not laugh or make fun of us. Stop stalling.*

After removing his glasses and spreading his female's legs wider, he nuzzled one thigh and then the other, more than a little surprised at how much the scent of her arousal affected him. He'd never really understood the other dragon-shifters and their talks of needing to taste someone. He'd put it down to them being sedated after surgery and spouting nonsense.

However, as he stared at Grace's center, wet and swollen, he leaned forward and gave a tentative lick. The taste of her sweetness hit his tongue with a tang of salt, and it shot straight to his genitals.

His beast growled. *Cock. Pussy. Use the words. And taste her, drive her wild. I'm being patient, but she's right there. Don't hold back.*

One of Grace's fingers ran through his hair, and he gazed upward to meet her eyes. Her lovely brown eyes were heated, half-lidded, but also a tad...impatient, he thought.

Someday, he'd be able to read her emotions as easily as reciting the periodic table.

His dragon growled again. *Stop procrastinating. Focus on our female. Make her scream out in pleasure and call our name.*

He wanted that, more than anything. To be the male Grace wanted above others, for more than his name and protection.

So he focused on her...pussy. Licking and lapping, using how she dug in her nails or pushed his head closer to judge what she liked. A light swirl, a longer lick, and then he took her clitoris between his lips and suckled.

"Trahern, yes. Oh, yes. Harder. Please."

He continued to swirl and then suckle as he dared to put a finger inside her.

Grace was warm and wet and tight, and for the first time in his life, he wanted to put his...cock...inside her. To claim her. Enjoy her. And then do it again and again.

His dragon hummed. *Yes, yes, she is our female. Our mate. Next time, we'll claim her with our cock. For now, make her scream and taste her orgasm.*

As he moved his finger, in and out, he tried lightly nibbling his female. Grace's thighs tightened around him as she cried out and relaxed. Her inner walls tightened and released as her orgasm played out, and he continued gently kissing and licking her bundle of nerves until she slumped against the ground.

His beast growled, *Taste her.*

After removing his finger, he lapped at her entrance, groaned, and then thrust his tongue inside her core. There was no reason he should savor her sweet saltiness, and yet he did. Maybe because it was proof she desired him.

Then he wondered how many more times he could make her orgasm with his mouth. How much quicker she could come for him. Maybe he could figure out exactly what she wanted, almost like an equation.

So Trahern kissed each of her inner thighs, pressed them wide, and started devouring his female all over again.

After her third orgasm, Grace finally convinced Trahern to stop torturing her core and kiss her lips again. As he explored and conquered her mouth, she gently stroked his hard cock through his trousers and waited to see how he reacted.

But he didn't flinch or move away. No, his pupils flashed a few times, so she did it again. Then she blurted, "I want to use my mouth, too. On you."

He stared at her, his pupils flashing more rapidly than she'd ever seen. His voice was husky as he replied, "We'll try. I want to feel you, but I'm unsure if it'll be too much sensation for me to handle."

Tracing his jaw, she searched his gaze. Tenderness rushed through her at the mixture of desire and uncertainty.

She kissed him gently before saying, "The last thing I want is to overwhelm you. Just tell me to stop at any time, and I will, Trahern. But at least let me try." She dared to stroke him and asked, "You like that, right?"

"Yes," he eked out before groaning.

Continuing to caress him, but slowly increasing the pressure, she watched his eyes. However, there was no panic—just desire, trust, and a sense of urgency.

Considering Trahern had to be about thirty and had never been with a female sexually, she didn't expect him to last long the first time.

First time. Trahern Lewis would be hers alone, and she rather liked that.

She kissed him and whispered, "My turn."

After nuzzling his cheek, she moved her mouth over his neck, his chest, down the trail of hair to his waistband, until she could kiss the outline of his hard cock.

"Grace."

Her name was a plea, not panic. No, as she met his eyes again, wetness rushed between her thighs at his fiery gaze. Trahern was so different from any man in her past. And right now, he looked at her with reverence. She also thought he cared for her, at least a little.

Maybe it was because she was caressing his dick, but she liked to think it was more than that. Maybe his feelings were starting to match her own, both in terms of trust and affection.

It would be easy enough to love this dragonman.

That thought should've scared her, and yet she knew Trahern wasn't anything like *him*.

Not wanting to dwell on her ex-arsehole, she instead focused on her mate, the male she hoped to be fully hers sooner rather than later.

So she undid his fly and pulled down the zipper. Maybe later she'd smile at his tight, white underwear. But for now, she focused on the straining material and pulled down the waistband to expose his cock.

Damn, her dragonman was long and thick and hard, so very hard.

And mine, rang through her head.

Not wanting to dwell on the latter, Grace ran a fingertip over the head, rubbing the drop of moisture around and around, until another appeared.

Trahern clutched the blanket with his fingers, his husky voice garnering her attention as he said, "Please, Grace. Touch me. I will orgasm soon, and I want to feel your fingers on me first."

She licked her lips, and Trahern's gaze zeroed in on her mouth.

Oh, he wanted more than her hand but probably didn't know how to ask.

Slowly, oh so slowly, she lowered her mouth until she was an inch from his dick and blew. Trahern arched his hips. "Grace."

"Give me honesty, Trahern. What do you want me to do right now?"

His gaze darted to her mouth, and he hesitated.

Maybe to some, it would irritate them or make them want to roll their eyes at the thirty-something virgin.

And yet, tenderness and a sense of protectiveness coursed through her. It was exactly because Trahern was different that she felt safe around him, cared about him, wanted a future with him.

Her unique dragonman was hers to claim.

So she took the first step. "I want to take your cock into my mouth, Trahern. Okay?"

He let out a strangled sound as his pupils flashed rapidly, then he nodded.

Grace focused on kissing the tip first, teasing the slit there with her tongue, and loving how her dragonman jumped and squirmed. And then she finally took him into her mouth.

One of his hands went to her hair, and he gently pushed her head, which she took as a sign to keep going.

Grace wrapped one hand at the base and squeezed. He thrust upward, and she managed to swallow his cock a little deeper. Once she was sure Trahern wanted more, she moved, up and down, learning how firm he liked it, how much tongue twirling he desired, and how wild he went whenever she paid extra attention to the tip.

Far sooner than she'd like, Trahern tugged on her hair. "Grace. I can't hold back. I'm going to orgasm."

She wanted to draw his cock deeper, but she respected his wishes and released him. Trahern took his dick, stroked once, and came hard onto his belly. She watched his face, the mixture of ecstasy and surprise making her think he wouldn't run or push her away.

When he finally slumped and closed his eyes to catch his breath, she brushed some damp hair off his forehead. "You all right, Trahern?"

"Yes. I just...need a minute."

She took out a wet wipe from the diaper bag, cleaned him up, and then lay down next to him. Trahern pulled her across his chest, and she snuggled close, smiling.

As Trahern stroked Grace's back, reveling in the feel of her head against his chest, he tried to catch his breath.

While he'd experimented with orgasms by his own

hand a few times, none of those compared to his mate pleasuring him with her mouth.

And judging by his penis already hardening again, he wanted more. Much more.

His dragon spoke up. *Cock. Our cock is hard. But yes, Grace's mouth is heaven. It will be even better when we claim her pussy.*

His...cock...turned to stone at the thought.

Was he ready? Could he claim his mate? Would she want it?

He asked his dragon, *Even if I attempted it, would you be able to hold back, still? I need to be in control the first time, I think.*

His beast paused, and then replied, *I think so. Although not much longer after that. I don't need a frenzy. That could hurt our mate since she birthed the twins not long ago. But I would need to claim her, too.*

Grace's voice snapped him out of his head. "Did you like everything I did? If not, you need to tell me."

His hand traveled down her back until he could rub one of her bum cheeks. He'd never really enjoyed touching before. But Grace was soft and warm, and he felt more connected to her whenever he was skin-to-skin.

Maybe they should always sleep naked. And together. He would sleep better with her pressed against him.

"Trahern?" She lifted her head, and he didn't like her furrowed brows.

He replied, "Yes, I liked it. All of it. I like you,

touching you. Just like with kissing, I think I need to practice with you. A lot."

She smiled and laid her chin against his chest. "Practice what? Do you mean shaking hands?"

He gripped her butt cheek. "No."

"Hmm. Maybe sitting together, holding hands?"

His fingers traveled upward, until he could tickle the top of her breast. Grace laughed and rolled onto her back. "That tickles, Trahern!"

He rolled to his side and danced his fingers over the top of her breast again. She tried to get away, and he followed, until Grace laughed and stopped him with a kiss.

Trahern devoured her mouth with his tongue and had just started moving a hand between her thighs when he heard one of the boys squirming. Grace couldn't hear it yet with her human hearing, but the twins would awaken soon.

Pushing aside his disappointment—the twins were important to him too—he eased his kiss until he could cup Grace's cheek and look at her slightly blurry face, wishing he had his glasses on. Regardless, he said, "I won't claim you fully yet. But I want you to sleep in my bed with me, Grace. And be naked."

She stroked his jaw. "The twins still wake up several times a night. They're getting better, but it's going to be a few months, probably, before they sleep through until morning."

"I will help you with them. But I want to feel you next to me, Grace. Please."

She smiled, kissed him gently, and nodded. "Okay."

Triumph surged through him just as one of the boys —he thought Eli—started crying. He said, "I'll check on him whilst you get dressed."

As he changed both boys and then helped Grace to feed them, Trahern nearly hummed. He might not have had a real family growing up, but he had one now. And they'd become part of his routine, one he'd take seriously forever.

Chapter Thirteen

The next morning, Grace's brain slowly woke up, until she could make herself blink her eyes open.

She was snuggled next to something solid and warm. After looking up to see Trahern still asleep on his back, she smiled.

He looked peaceful and younger, free of trying to maneuver in a world that didn't see things in quite the same way as him.

But what some would label quirks, she only thought of as parts that made up her mate—the dragonman she was falling for.

Between offering to help with the twins during the night and his tender way of holding her close and kissing her gently before telling her to go back to sleep afterward, Grace had struggled not to cry.

Not because she was sad or upset. No, Trahern was

the sweetest man she'd ever known. And when combined with how he could make her come quickly—he'd demonstrated twice more yesterday using his mouth again before they'd gone to bed—she still had trouble believing he was hers. How had no one snatched him up before?

As she reveled in her dragonman's heat and scent, Grace realized she was happy. It was a strange feeling after so many months of misery and worry inside the prison. And yet, she woke up each day wanting to talk with Trahern, to learn more about him, and to watch as he played with her boys.

No—their boys, she corrected.

Despite everything Trahern had done, though, Grace still struggled to believe her happiness would last. She wanted it to. Oh, how she wanted it to. However, her track record wasn't great. The last time she'd thought she cared for a man, it'd ended in disaster.

Trahern's voice, rough with sleep, garnered her attention. "You tensed up. Why?"

Since they'd decided to keep the boys in her old room—which was next to his, so they could easily hear them in the night—and didn't have to worry about waking them, she replied honestly, "Because I'm happy. And in my experience, that means it'll vanish soon." She paused, and as if sensing she needed a minute, Trahern waited. Eventually she replied, "The last time I thought I was happy, I was betrayed."

He rubbed his hand up and down her back, and she relaxed a fraction.

After about a minute, Trahern's voice rumbled under her cheek. "What happened, Grace? Tell me."

She hesitated, playing with the hair on his chest. Could she tell him? She didn't want to taint their newly-developed closeness. And sharing about how desperately she'd wanted to be loved, to the point she'd overlooked all the red flags from her ex, would make her look the fool.

Then she remembered Trahern had shared the most embarrassing moment of his adult life, when he'd attempted to have sex for the first time. He'd trusted her, and now it was her turn to do the same.

Even if she couldn't quite look into his eyes yet, she replied, "I told you about my mum and my stepdad, and how that ended. Afterward, I was hesitant to trust anyone and kept to myself more than was good for me. A little over a year ago, there was a new woman at my job, a fellow employee, and she was nice. We talked and even laughed sometimes. She encouraged me to go out and have some fun. Just some drinks and maybe some dancing with a few random guys. The more I went out, the more relaxed I became, and I started to enjoy it. I went out and danced as often as possible, and one guy charmed me. I didn't know he was a dragon-shifter at first since Cardiff—where I was living at the time—had strict rules about dragon-shifters socializing at night."

The first time she'd seen his pupils flash, when

they'd been alone walking to get a takeaway after a night of dancing, she'd nearly jumped.

However, as he'd continued to charm and tease and compliment her, his being a dragonman hadn't mattered. Like most humans, she'd heard the rumors and tales of how awful they could be. But he'd been...different. Or so Grace had thought.

Trahern squeezed her waist, bringing her back to the present, and she continued, "He confided in me about living just outside Cardiff, away from any dragon clan, since he was training to be a doctor. He commuted into the city and found it easier to pretend to be human."

After grunting, Trahern replied, "Cardiff University is one of the few that allow dragon-shifters to study there. But I somehow doubt he was."

"No. I didn't learn that until much later, though. Instead, I was so desperate to be loved, relishing in his attention and care and desire, that I didn't push when he brushed off my questions about his studies, or his family, or where he was from since his accent wasn't Welsh. Before I ever learned the truth, I found out I was pregnant."

It'd been a shock when the stick had told her that. Grace had tried to be careful, both with condoms and birth control pills.

Only later had she learned how the dragonman had switched out her pills with placebos and had used deliberately tampered condoms.

His goal had been to impregnate her as soon as possible.

Needing Trahern to understand the rest, she continued. "As soon as I told him, a satisfied glint entered his eyes. Not surprise or panic, but as if he'd planned it all along. I confronted him, and he gloated, saying he had switched out my birth control pills and poked holes in the condoms. When I asked why he'd done that, his entire demeanor changed. Gone was the charmer, and his eyes turned cold and calculating as he said he did it for money.

"Confused, I tried to run away, but that's when he took out a syringe and filled me with something to knock me unconscious. When I woke up, my brain was still hazy, but I overheard him asking when he'd get the rest of the money for the baby. After some more words I could barely make out, he was gone, and I was locked up inside that prison. They told me little beyond that if I didn't behave, they'd restrain me to ensure I didn't harm myself or the baby I carried."

Her voice cracked toward the end, and Grace closed her eyes, willing herself not to cry. Even now, being free and in the arms of a dragonman she actually admired, the fear of something happening to her and her children threatened to break her.

Trahern's strained voice filled her ears. "They're looking for him now, Grace. I won't stop asking Bram and Kai until they catch him. You deserve to feel safe and free of fear."

Opening her eyes, Grace moved her head so she could meet Trahern's gaze. His pupils flashed rapidly, and combined with his clenched jaw, he was the closest to angry she'd ever seen.

She placed a hand on his cheek and caressed his skin with her thumb. "I feel safe with you, Trahern."

"I'm not a Protector or soldier, though."

"No. But I trust you, which is something I never thought I could do with any man again."

His expression softened a fraction. "I vow to try my best to honor your trust."

Smiling, she moved until their faces were level. "As long as you continue to be your honest, quirky, clever self, that's enough." His face flushed a little, probably from embarrassment, and Grace murmured, "Kiss me, Trahern."

And he did, worshipping her all over again before the twins stirred and he had to go to work.

Chapter Fourteen

A few days later, Trahern struggled to analyze the data on his computer screen. Memories of the morning, when Grace had taken his cock into her mouth, kept surfacing.

With each passing day, he grew more and more comfortable with being naked and touched and touching in return. So much so that he wondered if he was ready to finally claim his mate completely.

His dragon sighed. *Please say you are. I can't have her until after you, since I promised. And I want her.*

Maybe.

Well, just imagine if another male tried to claim her. How does that make you feel?

He mentally growled. *She's ours.*

His dragon sounded smug. *She is. Make it official. Although you might want to take a few days off.*

Why?

Because once you experience it, and claim Grace, you'll want to do it over and over again.

How do you know? Neither of us has had sex before.

Trust me.

And strangely, Trahern did.

He and his inner beast had come a long way over the past few months. In taking Grace as his mate, he'd helped himself just as much as he'd helped her.

As he puzzled over fate and whether there was a way to scientifically prove it, someone knocked on the door of his research lab. Pushing aside thoughts of Grace and fate and everything else, he said, "Come in."

Dr. Scarlett Turner walked into the room, and he stated, "I didn't know you were visiting."

"It's unexpected. But we need your help, Trahern."

"Why? What happened?"

As she explained about one of her current patients—a young dragon stuck in his dragon form and recently operated on by some dragon hunters—and how they had been testing mind control equipment, he quickly focused on the details. He asked questions, and by the end he stated, "If you send me the information you have, I'll work on it straight away."

Dr. Turner shook her head. "No. The information is too sensitive. I need you to come with me, Trahern. To an undisclosed location."

"Ideally, I'd like to work here. But as long as there is a secure space—which Antony Holbrook always seems to have—then I can tell Grace to pack, and we'll be ready by tomorrow."

Dr. Turner's expression changed, but he couldn't quite determine the emotion.

She shook her head. "Grace and the twins can't come. It's highly sensitive."

"Grace would never share secrets."

The dragonwoman smiled at him. "I know that. But it's easier to sneak one person in without distracting attention than a group, especially if there are children."

"I can't leave Grace and my sons."

The doctor studied him a second before replying, "All of Stonefire will be here to protect her. And sticking to the facts, this young dragon will probably die if you can't help us."

According to Dr. Turner, the small mind control device had been surgically implanted into the young dragon's brainstem. While they didn't know everything, the current hypothesis was that the device kept the human half contained, preventing it from wresting back control from the dragon half. Both parts together made a dragon-shifter stronger. However, if forcibly kept apart, the dragon would rely on instinct more and more, until possibly losing any shred of human influence.

It was a dangerous thing, at least judging from dragon-shifters who had gone rogue before. The thought of a child suffering in such a way didn't sit right with him.

And yet, he couldn't abandon Grace.

His dragon spoke up. *As long as we ensure she is protected, and Kai increases security, she should be fine.*

Being away from his female would be difficult, especially as she'd become an intricate part of his routine.

And yet, the thought of a child maybe dying when he could help made his stomach churn.

Dr. Turner's voice was softer as she said, "I know it's difficult to leave someone you love behind, even for a short while. But all of Stonefire will guard your mate and sons whilst you're away. I can even ask Antony Holbrook to send someone to help guard her, if you agree."

He wanted to deny he loved anyone but couldn't. Why? He couldn't love Grace yet. Or ever, according to his father.

His dragon said softly, *He was wrong.*

"Trahern?"

Pushing aside his confusion about his emotions, he focused on the present. "I need to talk with Grace first."

The dragonwoman nodded. "Of course. Come find me after you talk with your mate. I'll be in the Protector building, talking to Antony about increasing security."

Instead of pointing out that he hadn't said yes yet, he merely nodded, stood, and exited. Since it was his designated research day and he didn't have any patients, he slipped out the back and headed toward his cottage.

Throughout the entire walk, he did his best not to think about how much Grace meant to him. For now, he needed to focus on maybe helping a child. Yes, that was his current task. Confronting his emotions could wait.

Grace was in the middle of folding laundry in the living room—she still couldn't believe how much washing she had to do for two tiny babies—when the front door opened and shut. Within seconds, Trahern stood in the room's doorway, his pupils flashing, and she asked, "Is everything okay?"

"No, there's a dragon child that needs my help. But it means leaving you and the boys here. Alone."

She went to him and didn't hesitate to touch his jaw. "Tell me everything, and then we'll discuss it."

After a few seconds, he replied, "Some acquaintances found a research facility run by the dragon hunters."

As Trahern proceeded to tell her about the place where they'd been running brain implant experiments on captured individuals, she sat down on the sofa and did her best to tamp down memories of her own imprisonment. She was free, and safe, and here with Trahern.

A hand on her shoulder snapped her out of her head, and she met Trahern's concerned gaze. "Are you all right, Grace?"

She shrugged. "It's difficult to hear about another prison run by dragon hunters. But before you say you won't ever share again, just know that I don't want to shy away from hearing about them. Besides, maybe my experience can help others." She placed her hand over his and squeezed. "What do they need you to do?"

He searched her gaze for a second before saying, "There is a young dragon stuck in his dragon form. The dragon hunters put a mind control device in his brain, and some of the doctors looking after him need my help in figuring out a way to either counter it or remove it without killing him."

The thought of one of the young dragons she'd seen around Stonefire being used as a test subject made her heart squeeze. "Do you think you can help him? Maybe even save him?"

"I don't have any of the details yet, so I'm unsure. But if capturing dragon-shifters and controlling their minds is the next phase of the dragon hunters, I need to help find a way to stop or at least reverse it. But..."

"But what?"

He traced her cheek. "I don't want to leave you, Grace. I promised to protect you and the boys."

Grace stood and gingerly placed a hand on Trahern's chest before leaning against him. The feel of his solid arm around her waist grounded her, helping to chase away the fear of her ex somehow finding a way onto Stonefire and stealing her sons. "We can ask Kai or Nikki to increase security, right?"

Trahern grunted. "Dr. Turner also said she'd get you additional security, from the secret branch she works for."

Grace tilted her head. "Secret branch? What are you talking about?"

Trahern briefly explained about the group of humans and dragon-shifters who worked together inside MI5, but technically didn't exist. And how they sometimes helped the dragon clans since their goals often aligned.

Once he finished, Grace asked, "So this bodyguard-type person would be one of those spies?"

"I'm not sure 'spy' is the correct term. However, yes, the person would be."

She traced his jaw, kissed him briefly, and pushed down her selfish desire to tell him to stay. "Then you need to go and help. No child deserves that fate, and you need to see if you can save him."

His eyes searched hers, full of doubt. He opened his mouth, but she placed a finger over his lips and said, "We'll be waiting here for you when you get back, Trahern. On top of the extra security, I also have Dawn and the other humans to ask for help. That poor child needs your cleverness, along with the others who were experimented on against their will." She paused, took a deep breath, and added softly, "After all, that's what they'd planned for Eli and Eddie."

Some of what the guards had talked about made more sense now. They had wanted to use her sons for the same experiments since they'd discussed mind control.

Trahern caressed her cheek, and she removed his finger. He whispered, "I won't let them get our sons."

Just hearing him refer to Eli and Eddie as "our sons" made her heart warm. She loved this dragonman and knew she could trust him with her and the twins' lives.

Not that she was ready to share her feelings. She wouldn't distract her dragonman right before he needed to leave and help a suffering boy.

She nodded. "If you trust these people who'll send extra help, then I do, too." She paused and then asked, "But will you be okay with the drastic change in your schedule and routine?"

"The only parts I'll miss are the ones with you and the boys."

Smiling, she caressed his jaw. "You're such a sweet man, Trahern Lewis, and I'm glad you're mine." He hesitated, and she kissed him gently. "Help the poor dragon child. I promise I'll be okay."

After a few long seconds, her dragonman nodded. "Okay. But I want two video calls a day. More if you need me, Grace."

"Done. When do you have to leave?"

He pulled her closer and nuzzled her hair. "Probably later today or tomorrow morning. I need to talk with Dr. Turner some more."

So soon. But no, Grace wouldn't be selfish in this. She knew what it was like to be a prisoner and mistreated. And for them to have experimented on a child? That was bloody awful.

And given her brilliant mate, he might be one of the few who could help save the dragon child with some kind of magical serum or concoction.

She held her dragonman tightly, breathing in his scent, and murmured, "My only requirement is that you spend a few hours with me and the boys before you leave. We'll even take lots of pictures and videos, so you can keep us close."

Grace had learned early that Trahern usually hated being photographed, let alone recorded. However, he nodded. "I want some with us all together. I want to keep my family close."

"Oh, Trahern."

Pulling his head down to hers, Grace kissed him, letting him know how much she'd miss him while he was gone.

Saying with actions what she couldn't quite bring herself to say with words.

Chapter Fifteen

Katrina "Trina" Lau parked her car in front of Stonefire's Protector building and took a few deep breaths.

This day had been coming for a while. She'd known it. And yet, meeting her half-sister face-to-face for the first time still made her heart race.

Stop it. You've survived serving in the army and Antony's training. This will be a walk in the park by comparison.

And yet, she had to take a few more deep breaths to calm down.

Trina had only learned about Nikki's existence a little over a year ago. Not from her mum—who was also Nikki's biological mother—but from her boss, Antony Holbrook. He'd warned her about Nikki Hartley-Gray the first time Trina had worked with Stonefire. However, while she'd met her brother-in-law, Rafe Hartley, she'd never met Nikki.

Nor had she told Rafe about who she really was, either.

Today, however, she would stop hiding. The last thing she needed was for someone to find out her connection, tell Nikki, and have her half-sister distrust her forever.

What I wouldn't give to tackle a dragon hunter to the ground right now to get out this excess energy and calm the hell down.

Her assignment this time, however, was to look after Grace Lewis and her twin boys. There was a dragonman who wanted to sell the boys to the hunters, even though he was their biological father.

The world was fairly fucked up sometimes.

Channeling her disdain and disgust at anyone willing to sell their child, Trina finally tamed her racing heart and put on her usual cheerful mask. Some of her male co-workers preferred scowls or menacing looks to intimidate. However, Trina was only human and of average height at best, and relied more on having others underestimate her.

Gathering her mobile phone and bag, she exited the car and headed to the building's entrance. Once inside, she gave her name and was shown to an empty conference room. Too full of energy and anticipation to sit, she stood and studied the room out of habit. A table, chairs, a two-way mirror, and at least two discreet hidden cameras. She quickly calculated how long it'd take to use a chair to break the glass versus picking the door lock.

In her line of work—unofficially a secret agent for the British government—a person always looked for an exit.

By the time someone knocked on the door, Trina had formulated three exit strategies. However, as soon as the door opened, she focused on the dragonwoman who entered.

While taller than Trina, Nikki was short for a dragon-shifter. She had light tan skin, black hair, and brown eyes. While Trina's were a darker brown, the shape was similar, as was her nose.

Her half-sister smiled at her, unaware that her life would change in the next few minutes.

Not that Trina knew how Nikki would take it.

The dragonwoman said, "Sorry to keep you waiting. We're grateful for your help, and Rafe had only good things to say about you." She put out her hand to shake. "I'm Nikki Hartley-Gray, second-in-command of Stonefire's security."

Trina shook and replied, "I'm Trina Lau. As I'm sure your mate told you, I work for Antony Holbrook."

"Yes, I'm quite jealous of Rafe, honestly. I had a long recovery after the birth of our second daughter, and he got to work with Holbrook instead of me."

The grumbly tone nearly made Trina smile.

Although the mention of the nieces she'd never met

reminded her of how she needed to be honest with Nikki. And quickly.

"Yes, well, Antony is exacting but fair. And with a dragon Protector as his mate now, he's more determined than ever to help the dragon-shifters as much as possible."

"I'm glad he and Iris found each other. By all accounts, they could run the UK if they put their minds to it."

Trina snorted. "Don't tell him that, or it'll go to his head. Antony needs a big ego to do what he does, but that doesn't mean we should encourage him."

Nikki gestured for her to sit. Although once Trina sat, she resisted jostling her legs under the table.

The dragonwoman studied her a second, her pupils flashing to slits and back before asking, "Why are you nervous? From what Rafe told me, you have nerves of steel."

Trina had rehearsed what to say a million times during her drive to Stonefire. And yet, all she blurted was, "My mother was Li-Na Wu."

Nikki blinked. "Pardon?"

"Your mother is my mother. We're half-sisters."

Silence stretched before Nikki replied, "She was never my mother." She stood. "I think it's better if you work with Rafe or Kai. I'll fetch one of them."

Before Trina could say another word, Nikki fled the room, the door clicking quietly behind her.

Only in a handful of her imagined scenarios had she

projected Nikki would welcome her with open arms. More of them had been full of rejection or resentment or hatred.

She knew only the bare bones of how their mother had been Stonefire's first sacrifice, and how Li-Na had fled as soon after the birth as she'd been able to.

And apparently, Nikki was going to hold their mother's actions against Trina.

Not that she'd let it interfere with her job. Nor would she give up that easily.

Nikki needed time, and Trina was patient.

And so she started to plan a new strategy of how to better know her sister if Nikki eventually wanted anything to do with her.

Chapter Sixteen

After a week of studying notes, prototypes recovered from the prison, and any records related to the dragon-shifters who hadn't survived the brainstem implant, Trahern was close to figuring out a way to help the young, sedated dragon in the next room.

Surgery would be risky, and his last resort. However, his latest test with a recovered prototype was promising. He'd been able to disable the device with a strategically placed needle. Whether by design or not, he'd discovered the millimeter-wide weak point. If he destroyed that spot on the microchip, it would no longer be able to receive instructions or commands from the software designed by the dragon hunters.

The only unknown, which was a major one, was whether the human half could rein in the dragon side once the device was disabled.

The young dragon was one of the two surviving prisoners from the experimental facility. Since the other person was in a coma, Trahern wouldn't be able to judge if his procedure worked or not.

However, the idea of risking the boy and getting something wrong made him uneasy.

His inner beast spoke up. *Each day he grows weaker from the sedatives. If we don't do something soon, he'll die.*

While they'd been able to silence his dragon with the dragon-silent drug, the boy wasn't responding well. Without the human half to help keep them together, the child was fading fast.

As Trahern went over his notes and findings yet again—he needed to be ready at a moment's notice, if the boy's condition worsened—Dr. Scarlett Turner walked into the room.

Of all the doctors inside the facility, he enjoyed working with her the best. She didn't chatter unnecessarily, spoke bluntly, and didn't seem to get annoyed with his quirks of needing to clean up his space or talk to Grace and the boys at exactly the same times every day.

Grace. He missed his mate more than he'd ever thought possible. For a male who'd spent his whole life avoiding touch and closeness, he was struggling to go without now that he wanted to claim his female.

Thankfully, Dr. Turner spoke and distracted him from his longing for Grace's touch. The doctor stated,

"You have to try disabling the device today, Trahern. The boy won't survive until tomorrow."

As he stacked his notes into a neat pile, he replied, "The probability of him dying is still over 50 percent."

"It will be 98 percent if he receives another dose of the dragon-silent drug. And no, there's nothing else left to try. Dragon-shifters don't do well with sedatives to begin with, and we've exhausted new ones to try."

He'd have to add devising new types of sedatives for dragon-shifters to his list of projects.

The doctor waited, and he knew there was no choice —he would have to try to save the young dragon. "Is the rest of your team ready to act?"

"Yes. Some of the best medical minds in the country are in the room next to the boy's."

He nodded, stood, and went to the far side of the room to collect the necessary tools.

The other doctor spoke again. "No matter what happens, you're giving him his best chance, Trahern. Remember that." He nodded without turning around, and the doctor continued, "We'll need you to continue to work on these devices, no matter what happens today. Antony received intel that the dragon hunters are trying to even the odds by having their own dragon army since we can counter most of the drugs they've used so far."

The aim of the dragon hunters was to harvest as much dragon's blood as possible and sell it. Since it had far-reaching healing properties, humans would often pay anything to save a loved one.

While in a perfect world the dragon-shifters would help anyone who needed it, their blood was one of the few bargaining chips they could use once the humans had forced them off most of their land.

However, politics wasn't Trahern's purview. He would always help someone who needed medical attention, but the power dynamics between dragons and humans were his clan leader's prerogative.

Once he had what he needed for the procedure, he turned, but Dr. Turner didn't move out of his way. She asked, "Do you want to call Grace beforehand?"

Just in case something goes wrong, was left unsaid.

As much as he wanted to scream yes, he shook his head. "If I call at an unscheduled time, it'll worry Grace. And she doesn't need any extra stress."

"Yes, I heard about a sighting of her ex in the Lake District. But don't worry, Antony sent a few more people to help track down and capture him. He won't allow the arsehole to harm Grace or your boys."

Since Antony Holbrook hadn't given him a reason to distrust him yet, he merely nodded and said, "Now, let's go. The stronger the boy is, the greater the chance he'll survive. If he's as weak as you say, every minute counts."

With that, they exited and went to the preparation room next to the boy's cell. Trahern ensured the medical team was ready before sterilizing everything and thoroughly washing his hands. Once he had the gown and cap on, he nodded at the nurse who was going to help him. He stated, "Remember, as soon as I tell you to move to the opposite side of the room, you do so."

The male nodded. "Yes, Dr. Lewis."

He approached the small blue dragon, who appeared to be about eleven years old. His chest rose and fell, but slower than a healthy person.

Moving to behind the boy's head, Trahern ignored the broken horn and focused on the base of the brain. He'd memorized the earlier scan and found the markings he'd made previously.

After turning toward the tray table one of the staff had placed next to the boy, Trahern scanned until he found the right tool—a syringe with an extra-long needle. The serum would help calm the boy after he'd punctured the microchip affixed to his brainstem.

Once he had it in hand, he checked the boy's vital signs and noticed they were dropping. It had to be now, or he might not be strong enough to pull through.

"Be ready to move."

The nurse nodded, and Trahern found the markings he'd made on the skin, where he'd clipped a few scales earlier. He took three deep breaths to steady himself and then counted to ten before pressing the needle into the skin. He met the expected resistance—he'd found the chip.

After one more deep inhalation, he pressed with just enough force to pierce the chip but not the brainstem.

The dragon jerked a second and Trahern said, "Now."

The nurse ran to the other side as he injected the serum.

Trahern carefully removed the needle and waited. Thirty seconds passed, then thirty more.

Then the vital signs sped up, beeping, and the dragon opened his eyes. Groggily at first, but then he jumped up and roared.

Something wasn't right.

"Listen to your human half! Work together! Don't let him bully you now!"

For a second, he thought maybe the human half was starting to take control as the dragon stilled and shook his head.

But then he roared again and charged at Trahern.

He tried to dodge, but the jagged, broken horn pierced his back before tossing Trahern across the room.

And as soon as he collided with the wall, the world went black.

Chapter Seventeen

Grace had just followed Trina out of her cottage with the pram when Myla, a younger female Protector with ginger hair, ran into view. She skidded to a halt and blurted, "Grace, you need to come quick. Bring your boys. We need to get you off Stonefire."

Her heart froze. "He found us?"

The dragonwoman shook her head. "No, that male is in Keswick right now, being watched. But it's Trahern. Something's happened."

Her stomach dropped. "What?"

"Let's go. I'll share on the way. Trina needs to come too."

Grace glanced at Trina, but she shook her head. "I don't know anything, or I would tell you."

As the two women ushered her along, Grace asked, "Is Trahern still alive?"

Myla replied, "From what I know, yes. But he's in a bad way, and you're his best chance at pulling through."

A million scenarios played out in her head, ranging from the dragon hunters finding Trahern to him being attacked by a rogue dragon-shifter.

Stop it. No matter what, you need to keep it together. She blurted, "What do you mean in a bad way? Don't keep me in the dark about this. Please."

Myla looked sheepish. "Sorry. I can be dramatic, according to my mum. He was attacked and had to go into surgery. He pulled through but is unconscious."

Trahern. "How can I help him? I want to, of course, but I'm not a doctor."

"No, but you're his mate. And he's become father to the twins. If anyone can encourage him to fight and pull through, it's the three of you."

"Of course, whatever you need, whatever Trahern needs, I'll help in any way I can."

And yet, as she was herded into the Protector building and told to wait while they made their last-minute preparations to leave, a niggle of doubt entered her mind. She might love Trahern, but he'd never spoken of strong feelings for her. Desire, yes. She knew he wanted her that way. But she had no idea if he loved her, or ever would.

Maybe her presence wouldn't be strong enough of a draw to help him fight and survive.

Eddie fussed, and she picked up her son and gently jostled him up and down. "Don't worry, Eddie. We're going to do whatever we can to help your dad. That means you need to help, too. And help Mummy. Can you be good for the trip? Daddy is going to need us rested and calm once we arrive wherever we're going."

She'd resisted calling Trahern their dad, but he was. It didn't matter if it was his DNA or not, he'd done more for the twins than a lot of biological dads ever did for their kids.

Holding Eddie closer, she breathed in his baby scent and willed her heart to calm a fraction. Eddie had always picked up on her moods the most, and she needed to keep it together for him, Eli, and most especially Trahern.

After Trina and Myla had herded her into a van and started down a back road—their undisclosed location was secret and needed to remain that way—she focused on playing games with her boys and telling them stories until they fell asleep.

Then she stared out the window and willed for Trahern to keep fighting until she got there. Because she refused to let him die.

It was hours later when someone shook Grace awake. She blinked until Trina's face came into view. "What is it?"

"We're here. I'll look after your sons whilst you go see Trahern alone."

Even though the dragonwoman had been nothing but kind and supportive over the last week, Grace still hesitated.

Then the brown-haired form of Dr. Scarlett Turner came into view and she said, "This is one of the safest, if not *the* safest, places in the UK for dragon-shifters. I vow your boys will be safe, but I also recommend seeing Trahern alone at first." She paused, and then her voice softened. "That way you won't have to pretend for your boys."

As she stared into the dragonwoman's flashing eyes, Grace's gut said to trust her. After all, Scarlett had helped her to better understand Trahern and had always been there when she needed to ask a question or two.

Looking down at her sons, she murmured, "Be good for Trina, boys. I'll see you again soon."

Since they were still asleep, she resisted kissing them and followed Scarlett out of the enclosed parking garage and into a long corridor. It was full of nondescript doors with little windows in the top halves. However, most of them were covered on the inside with little curtains.

Only after they turned a corner and walked past three more rooms did Scarlet stop and turn toward her. Her voice was quiet as she said, "Trahern is weak after being mauled by a young dragon. Whilst Trahern's surgery was successful and his vital signs are mostly stable, he's not as in tune with his dragon half as most. So I'm uncertain if they'll work together to heal faster—the injury probably would've killed a human. Which is why we've brought you here. He cares for you, Grace. If anyone can help the two halves work together and get Trahern to pull through, it's you."

Her throat tightened, and she willed herself not to cry. The fact that Trahern was probably only alive because he was a dragon-shifter spoke volumes about his injuries.

Grace nodded. "Trahern and his dragon have been working together better, but I'll talk to him. Maybe they can hear me and focus on healing."

"There is just one more thing—if his dragon half fully takes control in this state, it won't be good. It might even hurt his chances. So make sure they're together, or at the very least, the human half is in charge. I do think the boys will help, but I wanted you to see him first and let out your emotions. It'll help you later, when you decide to bring your children to visit." Scarlett placed her hand on the doorknob. "Come on. I can see I'm scaring you, and that's not my intention."

The dragon doctor entered the room, and after a deep breath, Grace followed.

Within seconds, she spotted Trahern lying on the hospital bed. He was hooked up to various machines, with his upper body wrapped in a lot of gauze, or something similar.

The breathing tube was the worst, though. Because if Trahern couldn't breathe on his own, things were bad. Very bad.

Willing herself not to cry, she walked over and

reached for his hand but hesitated. She didn't want to hurt him.

Scarlett murmured, "Yes, you can take his hand, just be careful not to jostle him. I'll wait right outside the door, if you need me."

The dragon doctor gently patted Grace's shoulder and left.

Once they were alone, she gingerly wrapped her fingers around Trahern's and squeezed.

His hands were colder than normal.

After swallowing the emotion in her throat, she did her best to keep her voice steady as she said, "I'm here, Trahern. Please get better. The doctor mentioned something about how you and your dragon must work together. I need the two of you to get along. Not just for me, but also for Eli and Eddie. You're their dad, and they need you." She paused, squeezed his hand again, and whispered, "I need you. I love you, Trahern. Please don't leave me. I love you."

And then a sob escaped her throat, and the tears wouldn't stop, no matter how hard she tried.

Trahern felt as if he were floating in a vast darkness. Not quite outer space, but similar. There was no sound, no wind, nothing but a sense of weightlessness.

Every once in a while, something would touch his arm or shoulder but then disappear.

The entire time he floated in nothingness, he tried to recall Grace's face, to recall their sons, to remember the day he'd shown them his dragon.

And yet, he could never manage it. No faces, no voices, no smells.

Just pitch blackness.

In addition to his family, something niggled at him. Something he needed to remember, and yet he didn't know what.

After a long time—or so he thought, since he couldn't judge anything in the void—there was a sob. And then more crying.

Sounds he'd heard before.

From Grace.

Why was she crying?

And why couldn't he go to her?

There was a sound—her voice—and yet he couldn't make out the words.

And he wanted to. He needed to see Grace. To hold her and tell her how much he wanted her.

Cared for her.

He couldn't imagine living without her. Or the twins. They were his everything. Essential to his happiness, and more important than even himself.

Perhaps this was love? He didn't know.

And the thought of never finding out what love was, of never treasuring Grace as she deserved, sent a rush of irritation through him. Followed quickly by desperation.

He wanted his family.

An unknown presence brushed against him, but Trahern still couldn't see anything. The presence touched him again.

Then something wrapped around his middle and tugged.

Was it a dragon's tail?

Soon he was gaining momentum, moving faster and faster until he emerged into a bright light. He blinked, unused to it, and he collided with a large, solid form.

Trahern blinked until the form of his inner dragon sat nearby, hovering over him.

But how could they be together?

His dragon spoke up, the voice projecting inside his mind. *You were in the tunnels. I found you.*

What tunnels?

You must still be out of it. The tunnels all young dragons use to hide until we start talking.

Young dragons. Tunnels. Talking.

Flashes of research and visiting a young golden dragon in Scotland danced inside his mind.

Still unclear, Trahern asked, *Why was I in the tunnels? And why did you have to tug me out?*

Don't you remember? We were hurt. And unless we work together, Grace and the boys will be alone. We need to heal for them.

Memories flooded his mind.

Disabling the microchip. The younger dragon charging at him. Pain through his back and shoulder. Unconsciousness.

Grace's voice, as if coming from a great distance and through water, said something to the effect of, "Please, Trahern. I love you. Wake up so I can tell you."

Could it be true? Did Grace love him?

He still wasn't entirely sure of the meaning, but she meant so much to him. And he could now hear her crying, each whimper a stab to his heart.

He tried to reach her, to move to the front of his mind so he could force his eyes open.

And yet, he couldn't manage more than moving a few fingers or his arm.

He growled. *What's going on? Grace shouldn't cry.*

His beast replied, *No, she shouldn't. But we need to work together to exit this place. Otherwise, we won't be able to see Grace again, let alone hold her.*

What are you talking about?

Human halves rarely enter the tunnels of a dragon-shifter's mind, and it's difficult to exit. I don't know why you did it, but now we have to find a way out together. And it's going to take time.

He wanted to growl again in frustration. However, that wouldn't help him reach Grace and his sons.

Tell me what to do. You managed to exit this place when we were young.

It's changed a bit over the years. But if you ride on my back, we can move faster.

He stood slowly, noticing how most of the pain in his shoulder was gone.

Maybe he was on some sort of painkiller.

Taking advantage of it, Trahern managed to get on his dragon's back with a lot of help. His beast's tail steadied him to keep him from falling off.

Once Trahern was settled, his beast spoke up again. *You need to tell me if you're going to slip off or fall unconscious. It took me a long time to find you. I might not be able to do it again.*

And if he couldn't, they might never wake up.

Trahern tightened his hold around his dragon's neck. *I'll be honest and let you know if I need a break. For now, maybe we can judge where to go using the direction of Grace's voice.*

As long as she keeps talking.

Not wanting to think of how lost they might get without some sort of beacon, Trahern replied, *Then let's get moving.*

As Grace talked, they often paused and took a second to determine which direction to go. And while he still couldn't make out all the words, he treasured every one he could, using them to remain conscious and cling to his dragon's back.

Chapter Eighteen

Grace sat next to Trahern's bed with Eli in her arms as she fed him some supplemental formula.

She'd been here for hours and had gone through so many emotions—fear, sadness, outrage, desperation, and determination.

The latter had kicked in as soon as Trina had brought the twins into the room. Both Eddie and Eli had reached their arms toward Trahern's bed, clearly recognizing their father and wanting to say hello.

She'd gently let the boys touch his hand before one had started to fuss, and then the other, signaling they were hungry.

Eddie had fallen asleep after eating. However, even once Eli was full and burped, he still babbled and snuggled against her, as if knowing she needed the support.

Cuddling her son close, she slowly moved to sit on

the bed beside Trahern and traced his cheek. His face was mostly unscathed, apart from a few scratches, and the doctors had said it was okay to touch his hands or face.

But as she did it, Eli waved an arm toward hers, wanting to do the same.

Trahern had only become comfortable with the boys touching his face in the last week or so before he'd left. The memory of Eddie grabbing his nose and squeezing still made Grace smile.

She said softly to her son, so as not to wake up his twin, "You have to be gentle, Eli. Can you do that? Yes? Okay. But only with Mummy's help."

She rearranged her grip and lifted her son until she could take his hand with her free one and guided it to Trahern's cheek. Eli patted it gently, and she said, "Yes, we're waiting for Daddy to wake up. He was hurt pretty badly, but he knows we're here. And we just need to keep telling him to wake up."

More baby babble.

"Yes, I'm sure he'll show you his dragon again once he's healed. But no, you can't slide down the dragon's side until you're older. You can't even crawl yet!"

She swore Eli looked peeved, but she dismissed it. Grace doubted he truly understood her, no matter Trahern's theories about inner dragons learning language in the womb.

Eli grunted in frustration, wanting to tug Trahern's hair, so she pulled him back and blew against his neck.

Her son squealed, and she did it again before saying, "How about I tell you another of Daisy's stories? Even if some of them aren't quite finished, we have fun making up our own endings, don't we? Let's see. How about the one with the dragon girl who watches all of her friends start talking with their inner dragons and hers hasn't yet?"

And as she told the tale of the girl feeling like an outcast, wondering what was wrong with her, until she finds out she has two inner dragons—Grace didn't know if that was even possible—Eli settled and his eyelids drooped.

All the while she eyed Trahern, willing him to wake up and join in. Maybe to lecture about how impossible it was to have two inner dragons. Or if it were possible, then about how difficult it would be to manage and keep three personalities in harmony in one brain.

Or any other scientific interpretation of a children's story.

She missed his literalness. Sometimes it was irritating, but sometimes it helped her learn something about dragon-shifters she never would've thought to ask.

Oh, Trahern. Please wake up.

Not that she let her worry show. If her sons picked up on it, Trahern might too.

Trahern and his dragon stopped often to rest.

The network of tunnels and open spaces inside this pocket of his mind was both fascinating and never-ending.

Not for the first time, he marveled at how young dragons could navigate their way out. Yes, his dragon had said he'd used Trahern's inner voice to find him. But it still took a lot of intelligence and stubbornness to accomplish.

Even with Grace's voice filtering through often, there were times when it stopped and he and his beast had to rest.

Now was one of those times, and Trahern relaxed on his dragon's back and hated how tired he was. He was a mental figure, and yet he still experienced exhaustion.

His dragon snorted. *It's funny you still wonder about that. We've always been mental projections inside our minds. This is no different.*

I didn't understand how deep it went.

At least you can use this for your research.

Since Grace's voice hadn't returned, he asked his beast, *You never answered my question about before you exited the tunnels, found me, and we talked. Did you understand English earlier than me?*

I don't remember. That was a long time ago.

While it wasn't the answer he'd been hoping for, Trahern didn't let it deter him. He spent an untold amount of time devising new hypotheses and tests for when he was well again. It helped distract him from the constant yearning for Grace's voice.

Eventually it returned, along with some faint sounds of one of the boys.

His dragon stood, and they started in the same direction they'd been going for a while, sometimes entering pitch-black areas where his beast relied on instinct to guide them through turns and crevices.

Once they exited into another bright part, he blinked. There was a small lake surrounded by trees. And a fake-looking sky was above, one that was utterly still and silent.

Despite the bright light, it was eerie.

He asked, *Where is this?*

His dragon replied, *This is the exit, where we can return to the main part of your mind.*

How? Tall cliffs surround the lake.

We leave by going through the water.

He blinked. *Pardon?*

It's a test of determination, of how much you want to be united with your human half.

Pushing aside his skepticism, he said, *Show me what to do.*

His dragon walked to the lake's shore, and then onto the smooth surface. Although it wasn't really water—it was solid and held their weight.

Trahern asked, *What is this place? Can you give me any more details?*

This is the barrier between the two areas of your mind. Usually, the human half is unaware of its existence. So it's strange you're here, for sure.

He tucked that information away for later. *So how do we go through since it's solid under our feet? Is there a ritual or multistep process?*

Not a ritual, but more you need to have the determination to want to go through it. And before you ask, I had your voice to guide me through as a child.

But not now. Was that the only way you were able to get through? By using a voice guide?

His dragon grunted. *I think so. It was only when I got so lonely on this side that I finally tried to break through the lake. Eventually, I found myself on the other side.*

Trahern had never really thought about how solitary it must be for inner dragons as a child. Even if he'd been alone most of the time as a kid, he'd had the options of books or TV or going to school.

His inner beast hadn't.

Maybe there was a way he could help young dragons break through earlier. However, to do that, he needed to get out of here and wake up again. *So, do you have an idea of how to pass through the lake? Can I even exit it?*

You have to. Somehow, some way, we need to reach Grace and Eddie and Eli.

A flash of Grace's brilliant smile, as the sun danced off her glossy black hair, sent a rush of longing through him. Even more so as she waved Eddie and Eli's little hands at him in farewell, as she often did when he left for work in the morning.

His chest ached, almost as if he were missing something. Which was ridiculous as he was a mental projection.

After sighing, his beast spoke up again. *It's your love for Grace and our sons. Whilst it may be mental, technically, it can affect your body's responses.*

As he tried to digest this—his friend Emily had tried to explain that to him once, but he'd been unable to accept it at the time—a voice rough from overuse filtered through.

Trahern, if you can hear me, open your eyes. Each passing day makes the doctors worry. They try to hide it, but I can tell. Even the boys are fussier than normal, probably trying to figure out why you never move.

The catch in her voice shot straight to Trahern's heart. He said to his beast, *Let's try passing through the barrier. I can't bear Grace's sadness. I just can't.*

His dragon grunted. *Right, then let's give it a go.*

As they stood on the mirror-like lake, Trahern focused on the feeling in his chest—the sense of tightness and emptiness, and how much he wanted to hold Grace in his arms before playing with the boys again.

At first, nothing happened. The surface remained firm. But the more he accepted how much Grace meant to him, how much he believed he loved her—he still wasn't sure if that's what this all meant—the surface softened slightly.

Slightly, but still not enough.

Then Grace's voice finally stopped, replaced with crying, and a sense of urgency rushed through him.

Trahern focused on Grace and Eddie and Eli. He couldn't let them suffer. He needed them too, and wanted to be a better male. For them.

And for himself.

For his dragon.

His beast hummed and glowed faintly as they started to sink through the glass lake.

Don't panic, his dragon said right before they disappeared under the surface and returned to darkness.

Chapter Nineteen

Grace pinched the bridge of her nose and then drank more tea from her mug. After so much talking, she was losing her voice.

It'd been nearly three days since she'd arrived at this secret location. And while Trahern was breathing on his own now, not much else had changed.

Scarlett had just left with the boys, taking them to the childminder so they could sleep. Apparently, this super-secret facility had daycare.

If she weren't so tired and worried, she might've laughed.

Rubbing her face, Grace tried to hold back her tears. She needed to be strong for Trahern.

But after a few deep breaths, exhaustion—both mental and emotional—crashed over her. She was beyond worried at this point, especially since the doctors were getting anxious, and a sob escaped her throat.

Their best guess as to why Trahern remained unchanged was that either his human or dragon half was silent, meaning they couldn't work together. And if they didn't, and soon, then Trahern might never wake up.

Another sob broke free at the thought of never seeing Trahern use the periodic table of elements to calm her boys, or watch him try to master a perfectly round pancake, or even the way his kisses made her feel like the most beautiful person in the world.

Trahern needed to wake up. He just had to.

And while Grace should be a better person and not be so selfish, she wondered why the boy who'd done this to Trahern had shifted back to his human form and had started his recovery already. All while her mate might die.

Stop it. Don't blame the innocent child. He didn't know what he was doing. If anything, it's the dragon hunters' fault for using the boy as an experimental test subject.

Grace was tired, so tired. And as her sobs calmed, she tried to regain her composure. Sleep. What she needed was sleep. As she glanced at the cot in the corner of the room, she wondered if a nap would help settle her emotions before she went to visit Eli and Eddie.

Just as she stood and turned from the bed, she heard a groan. After whirling around, she saw Trahern's fingers wiggle.

"Trahern?" she breathed, almost afraid to hope.

He groaned again, and she was next to him in a flash.

His eyelids lifted and stared unfocused for a few seconds before landing on her face.

"Grace," he croaked.

With a sob, she placed a hand on his cheek. "Trahern, you're awake! Thank goodness, you're awake." She tried to smile but failed. "I want to keep you to myself, but I need to call the doctors."

"Wait. Tell you. Something."

His voice was weak, but she willed herself not to cry as she replied, "Then tell me, Trahern. What is it?"

"Love you. I think."

His brows came together, as if trying to figure out whether he did or not.

Maybe some people would be offended. But for a dragonman who'd grown up without any affection and had trouble reading emotions, Grace knew he struggled to make sense of it all.

Leaning down, she placed a gentle kiss on his lips. "I love you, Trahern. And we'll figure it out together, I promise. But I need to call the doctors so they can help you and make sure you don't fall back into a coma."

"Kiss me. One more time."

She did, and then laid her forehead against his. Just staring into his eyes, watching as they flashed, made her smile. "Your dragon is with you."

"Yes. Long story."

He moaned as if in pain, and Grace forced herself to stand and press the call button. Within seconds, Scarlett rushed into the room. As soon as she saw Trahern on the bed, eyes open, she smiled. "Hello, Dr. Lewis. Glad to see you're back with us."

The dragonwoman went to his other side, saw his flashing pupils, and nodded. "Good. Your dragon is back with you as well?"

"Yes."

"Right, then you should heal a lot faster going forward. But I need to ask some questions and run a few tests while you're still awake. Unfortunately, that means your family reunion with the twins will have to wait."

Grace took Trahern's hand in hers and squeezed. "Tell me I can stay with him."

"I don't see why you can't. It'll probably save Trahern some time later with explaining everything. But first..."

The doctor asked a series of questions about pain, wiggling of toes and fingers, and a number of other health-related things.

By the end, the dragonwoman nodded. "Between your answers and our previous scans, I don't think there was any permanent brain damage. However, we're going to monitor you closely for quite some time, just in case. And no, you won't be able to go back to work for a while, so don't even ask." Trahern grunted reluctantly—or so Grace thought—and the doctor continued. "Right, so with the most pressing matters out of the way, we need to figure out why your scans showed no dragon or human activity despite the fact both of you are here now."

And as Grace listened to Trahern explain about hidden mental tunnels and solid mirror lakes, her jaw dropped. There was still so much she needed to learn about dragon-shifters.

Although judging by Scarlett's questions, some facts had been surprising to her, too.

The longer the doctor interrogated Trahern, the more he faded, until Grace interrupted, "Trahern should rest. I think he's given enough information for now."

Scarlett didn't frown but smiled. "You're right, of course. It's just that our inner dragons rarely discuss the time before we first talk together, and now one of my friends has experienced it and can help us better understand young dragons? It's bloody brilliant." She cleared her throat. "But yes, he should rest. I'll have a nurse come in to check your pain medication, and I'll be back in a few hours. However, if Trahern crashes or acts out of character, alert me immediately."

Grace nodded. "I will, Doctor. I promise."

"Right, well, I'll go share what you've told me with the others. I'll be back later."

Once Scarlett left, Grace squeezed Trahern's hand in hers again. "You should rest."

"Not yet."

She arched an eyebrow. "Why not?"

"I want to hold you, Grace. Please."

"But I don't want to hurt you."

"You won't. If anything, it'll help me heal faster."

She somehow doubted that, but as he slowly moved

to one side—wincing a few times, the stubborn man—she caved. Gingerly, she laid down and rested her head on Trahern's uninjured shoulder before helping him move his arm to wrap around her. He gently squeezed and sighed, as if in relief.

As she traced shapes on his chest, she suddenly didn't know what to say. She'd been pleading for him to come back, and he had. She'd told him she loved him, and he thought he might love her, too.

And yet, she wondered if he'd said it in the heat of the moment? Telling her what she wanted to hear to calm her down?

After about a minute, Trahern spoke again. "Your voice guided me out of the tunnels."

"Hmm? Yes, you mentioned that."

"I don't think you realize how vital it was."

She tilted her head to look up. During the doctor's examination, she'd given Trahern his glasses back. Once she met his gaze, he continued, "Without you and the twins, I wouldn't have had a reason to come back. I might've stayed exploring the tunnels forever."

Even though her throat threatened to close up, she forced herself to ask, "Do you regret leaving them? I know how important your research is, and how much you could've learned by staying in those tunnels."

He frowned. "At one time, you would've been right. However, whilst I have a few new ideas for research, none of it is more important than you, Grace. No research ever will be."

Her eyes heated with tears. Maybe he *had* meant what he'd said earlier.

She wanted to kiss him senseless, but knew she couldn't. Not yet. So instead, she blurted, "I love you, Trahern. I'm so glad you offered and claimed me as your mate."

He almost smiled. "I haven't claimed you fully yet. But I want to, as soon as I'm healthy again." He squeezed her waist. "You mean so much to me, Grace. You and the boys. I think it's love, but I'll have to ask some friends to be sure."

"I can help, if you want to tell me why you think so?"

It was a risk, considering she would be honest with him and it might not be love after all.

And yet, she wanted Trahern to tell her. To see if it were true and that somehow, some way, she might've found the dragonman she trusted enough to spend her life with.

To be a father to her children, both to the twins and any they might have in the future.

To be her best friend and partner in all things.

So she waited, her heart racing, trying not to get her hopes up. She could be patient, although she'd be lying if she didn't want him to feel the same about her as she felt about him.

It was getting harder and harder to keep his eyes open, and Trahern needed to rest.

However, as soon as Grace had told him again that she loved him and was glad he'd claimed her, he'd woken up a little. Especially as he tried to determine his feelings.

Unlike most of his ordered world, he didn't have a guide to love.

His dragon spoke up. *Even though I know we love her, just tell her what you treasure about her, how she makes things better, all the little things that helped us escape the tunnels to be with her again.*

He hesitated before replying to his beast. *But what if she doesn't think that's enough?*

This is Grace. She will listen and talk with us and be honest. If you truly want to claim her fully once we're well, you need to talk about this now.

With Grace's heat at his side and her scent filling his nostrils, he tightened his hold around her. He wanted more, so much more, than to merely lie with her in his arms.

Not that he was well enough to do anything else.

But now that he desired her, wanted to claim her and have sex with her, he was impatient.

His dragon snorted. *You're starting to understand how I've felt all these years.*

Yes. Honestly, I never really understood it before. I'm sorry.

His beast grunted. *No worries. Talk with Grace. The*

longer you wait, the more she tenses up, as if bracing for
bad news.

Trahern had been so lost in conversation with his
dragon that he hadn't noticed. However, when Grace
tried to inch away, he tightened his grip on her. "Don't
leave."

"I should go. You're tired and need sleep, and I have
no right to ask you to lay out your feelings right now."

"No, Grace. It needs to be now. Look at me." Once
her eyes met his—was that a touch or wariness?—he
blurted, "I always want to be with you. I want to touch
you and kiss you and now even want to have sex with
you. And it's strange to me because I've never wanted to
tell a person everything before. And yet, I want to be
with you. I've told you about the humiliating parts of my
past, what my father was like, and you even try to learn
about what I'm researching, even when you've never
heard of a certain topic before.

"But you also helped me learn how to get along with
my dragon. That isn't romantic, from what I've overheard from others talking about love, but it's one of the
most important things. My beast and I learned to work
together so we could better know you. So we could help
you and make you smile and ensure you were taken care
of. To be more open and less reserved for Eddie and Eli,
to be the father they need. In short, together we might be
able to be the male you deserve."

"Oh, Trahern."

"It's true. I will always be a bit different from other

dragon-shifters, and that's something I can't change. But you've helped me understand that being different isn't a bad thing. And whilst the world may always be a little confusing for me, you make sense to me, Grace. So much so that I want to keep you with me always. So would you call that love?"

Her eyes looked a little wet, but before he could ask if she was going to cry, she cupped his cheek and whispered, "Yes, Trahern. And after hearing all of that, I can say you're one of the most romantic people I've ever met."

"Don't lie to me, Grace."

"I'm not. I can ask as many people as you like, and almost all of them will agree with me. I love you, Trahern Lewis. And as soon as you're well, I'm fully on board with deflowering you."

"Deflowering?"

She kissed him gently and said, "Taking your virginity and claiming you as mine."

His dragon roared. *Yes. We'd better get healthy fast. I want to have her on my own, too.*

"Both me and my dragon? Because he wants a turn, too."

She brushed some hair off his forehead. "Yes. After talking with the other human women, I'm actually curious about your dragon half. But I want you, the human part, first."

"I already made that agreement with my beast."

"Good." She kissed him again, and then snuggled

against his side. "I love you, Trahern. But we both need to rest so you can get better."

Exhaustion crashed over him, and he yawned. "Stay with me, Grace."

"Always, Trahern. Always."

And as he fell asleep with his female in his arms, Trahern felt more content and at peace than he ever had in his life.

Chapter Twenty

Nearly two weeks later, Grace and Trahern arrived back on Stonefire, each carrying a baby. While the clan had sent letters and cards and drawings for Trahern to get well—the students had coordinated it—they'd asked for everyone to allow them a few days alone before greeting the clan.

And so, Grace followed Trahern into their cottage, her body relaxing as the front door closed behind her. She'd only been on Stonefire for a little under four months, and yet it truly felt like home. Especially this cottage, where she and Trahern and the twins could be themselves, with no pressure.

Once they'd settled the twins on the floor in their little activity sets—little bars above them with dangling toys in bright colors and shapes—she said, "I'll put the kettle on."

Trahern nodded, but focused on the boys.

As she got the tea things ready, she tapped her hand against her thigh. Both she and Trahern had hummed with energy and impatience for days now, wanting to finally sleep together. Well, have sex together as she'd slept next to him many times over.

Would it happen today? And why was she so nervous?

Probably because she wanted Trahern's first time to be good, which put a lot of pressure on her.

Stop it. Just like with anything, no doubt practice would make perfect. And she smiled, thinking of how Trahern would suggest practicing a lot at first, to discover their own type of rhythm.

Once the tea was ready, she carried the mugs to the living room and sat next to Trahern on the sofa. Leaning her head on his shoulder, she merely sighed.

"Is something wrong?" he asked.

"No, it's just nice being home again. As much as I like Scarlett and the others, the four walls of your hospital room made me antsy. Even if we're merely sitting, just seeing the trees outside the window is a huge improvement and helps me feel more at ease."

He glanced at the large window. "I've never really thought about the view outside. Maybe we should start a small vegetable garden in the back, which you can see out of the kitchen window, and it'll also help the boys learn about germination, photosynthesis, and maybe even cross-fertilization."

"It's a good idea, but maybe wait until they can walk

first? Right now, they'll probably just eat the dirt and throw it around."

As they watched the boys reach for the toys and bat at them, or tug, or run a finger down a dangling giraffe, Grace snuggled more against her mate.

His arm went around her shoulders and tugged her closer before taking a deep inhalation. She bit back a smile but couldn't help but tease. "Are you sniffing me?"

"Not sniffing. The smell of your hair products soothes me."

"What if I changed to a different brand? Would you stop liking my scent?"

"Of course not. There is an underlying one that is purely yours. I should research more about how it was useful in the past, in early human and dragon-shifter evolutionary history, to identify a mate."

"Hmm, I wonder if the relationship between humans and dragons was closer thousands of years ago compared to now? Or worse?"

Trahern sipped his tea before replying, "I can ask Maximilian Holbrook and his mate, Dr. Lavinia Holbrook, and you could ask them your questions. They're both dedicated to human and dragon-shifter history."

She laughed. "I don't need a private lecture. I was just wondering, is all. Maybe I need some elementary dragon-shifter texts to help get me up to speed. I meant to do it earlier, but taking care of newborn twins doesn't really lend itself to loads of free time."

"I will get anything you need, Grace. Just ask me. Because I don't ever want you to feel adrift. You help anchor me, and I want to do the same for you."

She gazed up at her handsome mate. "I know, Trahern, and you do help anchor me." She kissed the side of his neck. "I love you."

He kissed her lips gently and maintained eye contact. "I love you, too." His pupils flashed a few times, and he asked, "When do you think the twins will be ready for a nap?"

"Oh, I don't know. Maybe not for hours yet."

He grunted, and she laughed. "I'm as eager as you, Trahern. Which is why I think it'll be best to have someone watch the boys for an evening. That way we won't be interrupted."

Which meant waiting some more.

And as Trahern kissed her again, frustration swelled. Grace didn't want to wait.

As she tried to think of who could watch the boys on short notice, the doorbell rang. With a sigh, she handed her mug to Trahern and went to answer it.

So much for having some alone time.

Although as soon as she opened it and saw Hayley standing there, wearing a grim expression, her stomach dropped. Grace blurted, "What is it?"

"I think I'd better come in and tell you and Trahern at the same time."

She gestured, and for the agonizing seconds it took to walk back into the living room, she refused to let awful scenarios play out in her head. Especially once she saw her boys still playing on their mats.

They were safe.

And yet, something was wrong.

Was her ex nearby? Or maybe there was a mistake on her DDA paperwork?

Wait and see before you worry.

Which was easier said than done.

Hayley motioned for Trahern to join them on the far side of the room. Once he arrived, Hayley stated without preamble, "The Department of Dragon Affairs has received a custody request for your twins. No, it's not from your ex but rather his mother."

She frowned. "I was told that she was dead."

"No, not dead, but living with a dragon clan in Portugal. She submitted DNA, and it was confirmed she's the twins' paternal grandmother."

Her heart thudded in her chest. "Surely they won't give her custody? Genetics doesn't instantly make a good parent or guardian."

Hayley shook her head. "No, of course not. But in her petition, she indicated Trahern wouldn't be a good father. Rubbish, of course. But she claimed he's mentally unstable and unable to stay focused when alone with the twins, making him a danger."

Trahern growled. "No. When I'm with them, they have my complete focus. In the early weeks, I struggled. But now? They and Grace are my reasons for still being alive."

Hayley replied, "I know that, and you know that, but rumors of your past haven't helped. Especially since the paternal grandmother brought in someone to help plead her case."

"Who?" Trahern asked.

"Your father."

Trahern had been debating whether he could ask Blake and Dawn to watch the boys—their friend Marianna had left Stonefire—when Grace returned with Hayley Beckett.

And then she shared the custody news.

But when the human female said his father was being a character witness against him, Trahern blinked and tried to process it. Years had gone by, and no one seemed to have spotted him anywhere. The only reports his former clan leader, Rhydian Griffiths, had shared suspected that he'd joined the clanless dragon-shifters living in Scotland.

Half of whom had been killed by dragon hunters not too long ago.

He'd surmised his father had been one of those murdered since he didn't—or hadn't?—possessed skills valuable for dragons living in the wild. His father had been an accountant, and not a good one, either.

His dragon spoke up. *We need to learn if it's truly him or not. If so, then Rhydian and the others who witnessed our father's actions back on Snowridge need to speak up.*

Which meant he'd have to ask for their help. *But we left Snowridge. Why would they help us?*

Rhydian wasn't like the older leader and always tried to understand our point of view. It was others inside the clan, the ones who are mostly banished to the outlying farms now, who made our life difficult.

A number of years ago, Rhydian's mate Delaney had been threatened and targeted by the anti-human dragon-shifters. Wanting to keep a close eye on them while still protecting his mate, Rhydian had put those clan members on isolated farms in northern Wales.

He replied, *That might be true, but will Rhydian's word be enough to counter our father's, if he is still alive?*

Maybe not, but if we ask all our allies and friends to help, it should be.

Trahern tapped his forefinger and thumb against each other, and Grace gently touched his upper arm, bringing him back to the present as she asked, "Is it possible your father is still alive? Or do you think it's an imposter?"

Hayley jumped in. "All dragon-shifters are registered with the DDA, so they confirmed the dragonman is in fact Trahern's father. However, the DDA is still sifting through his statements, according to Evie's DDA contacts. Regardless, a social worker is coming tomorrow to interview you both and ensure the boys are well."

Grace narrowed her eyes. "How dare they! My boys

are well-loved and cared for, and anyone on Stonefire can vouch for it!"

Hayley laid a hand on Grace's arm. "I know, Grace. The good news is that I've dealt with DDA custody battles before. And because of the database I've built, which is nearly done and mostly functional, I have a lot of former custody disputes and battles to pour through and use as precedent."

Hayley was a former solicitor and, together with her mate, Nathan Woodhouse, had been building a database of laws related to dragon-shifters in the UK. In the past, the decentralization of such information had made battling the DDA difficult. He'd always admired her initiative.

Trahern said, "I can help as well. No, I'm not a lawyer, but I'm good at spotting details, and I remember almost everything I read. It could help speed things up."

"Thank you," Hayley said with a smile. "I could use your help. But first, I need you to reach out to Snowridge and see who can give character statements for you, as well as who can confirm your father's past actions and behaviors. I don't know everything, but just his official DDA record alone tells me he's not a paragon of society."

Grace took his hand and threaded her fingers through his. "I can help you with anything you need, Trahern. Together, we'll win this. You'll see."

His clever, beautiful, strong mate. "My father has added yet another reason for me to dislike him."

"Because he's trying to rip apart your new family?"

"Yes, but also because it means I can't fully claim my mate tonight like I want to."

Grace kissed him, and Hayley looked away.

Once his mate pulled back, she whispered, "At least it gives us time to find someone to watch the boys for a night, right?"

He smiled. "Still looking for the bright side?"

"Someone has to."

As much as he wanted to tease his mate some more, he focused and asked Hayley, "What do I need to do? Tell me the order of importance and exactly what you're looking for from Snowridge, and I'll get started right away."

And as he, Grace, and Hayley formulated a plan, Trahern vowed to solve this as quickly as possible. His mate and sons deserved happiness, and he was determined to give it to them.

But first, he was going to put his past with his father behind him, once and for all.

Chapter Twenty-One

After ten days of nonstop activity and chaos, Grace sat in a large room next to Trahern, waiting for the arbiter to enter.

From what she'd learned from Hayley, the DDA ran the dragon-shifter custody hearings in lieu of judges. Which meant no wigs or robes or any of the traditional stuff she'd seen on TV shows.

Still, despite how her heart raced and palms sweated, Grace stole another glance at Trahern. He was always handsome, but seeing him in a suit made her want to drag him into a dark corner and have her way with him.

And yet, as he tugged at the top button again, she knew how the formal clothing didn't "feel right against his skin." However, Hayley had cautioned that to appear in his normal clothes would be disrespectful and might harm their case.

So Trahern had donned the clothes he described as scratchy, hot, and too tight.

He willingly made himself uncomfortable to help her and her boys.

Oh, how she loved her dragonman, for so many reasons.

Under the table they sat at, she took his hand and squeezed. His flashing eyes met hers, and she smiled.

Trahern stopped tugging at the button and squeezed her hand back.

Whispers from the back of the room garnered Grace's attention, and she turned to see a woman in her early 50s with light tan skin, black hair, and dark eyes walk up the aisle and sit down at the table on the opposite side.

She never once looked in Grace's direction.

However, she knew it was Madalena Silva, her ex's mother.

She nearly growled. But Trahern squeezed her hand again, reminding Grace that no matter how much she wanted to drag the dragonwoman outside and tell her to sod off, she wouldn't give her anything to use against them.

Soon after Madalena sat down, the door at the front of the room opened. They all stood as the panel of arbiters walked in, consisting of three men and two women. After they sat behind a long table—one on a dais raised six inches above the floor—everyone followed suit.

Grace's heart raced as she waited for someone to

speak. Eventually the man sitting in the center, with gray hair, dark skin, and dark eyes, put on a pair of spectacles and finally stated, "We're here to discuss the custody of Elijah and Edward Lewis. Are all parties present and ready to begin?"

She was about to reply in the affirmative when the doors at the back of the room opened. After turning, she gasped as the tall forms of Rhydian Griffiths, Wren Jones, and Dr. Maelon Perry from Snowridge took their seats at the back.

She whispered to Trahern, "Did you know they were coming?"

"No. They provided statements, but I said it was unnecessary for them to come in person."

The man at the front table cleared his throat, regaining control of the room. Once silent, he stated, "I will excuse your tardiness since my assistant tells me you came all the way from Wales. Now, let's begin. We're here today to determine the best homes for Elijah and Edward. Their paternal grandmother, Madalena Silva, has put in a request for full custody, based on the unsuitability of Dr. Trahern Lewis as a guardian. Dr. Lewis's own father has provided statements to bolster her claim, and will join us shortly to answer our questions. However, Mrs. Grace Lewis has refuted their objections and provided her own evidence and character witnesses for why Dr. Lewis is a suitable guardian. Since the burden of proof falls on Dr. and Mrs. Lewis to disprove the claims, Ms. Beckett, please begin your defense."

As Hayley cited various case law, as well as the criminal history of Trahern's father, and how Grace's ex had sold her to dragon hunters and would be a danger to the twins if his mother gained custody, Grace took strength from Trahern's hand in hers.

Trahern still tried to understand why Rhydian and the others from Snowridge had traveled to England. It would've taken considerable paperwork and time to get here.

His dragon spoke up. *They were our allies before, no matter how much you tried to ignore the entire clan.*

Before he could think of a response, Hayley called Rhydian to the front of the room. Once he sat in front of a microphone, Trahern focused on his former clan leader.

Hayley asked, "You're the current leader of Clan Snowridge in Wales, correct?"

"Aye. For many years now."

"So you're familiar with Trahern and his father, Dewi Lewis?"

"Of course. Even though Dewi left the clan years ago, I'm very aware of him. Especially as he's wanted by the clan for neglect of a child and attempted murder."

Trahern frowned. He'd never heard of this.

Hayley continued, "For neglect and attempted murder of his son."

"Aye. The former head doctor, Arwel Hughes, found high amounts of poison in Trahern's body as a boy, and was acquainted with Trahern and knew he'd never take the poison willingly or by mistake—he was a very clever lad with plants and science and such. However, whilst the former clan leader never addressed it, I take harm to a child seriously. Once I became clan leader and learned of it, I informed my head Protector to detain Dewi Lewis. That's when he fled Snowridge and never returned."

Trahern's head spun. Was it true? Had his father run away because he'd been wanted for a crime and not because of him embarrassing the male?

His dragon said softly, *He was an arsehole. I never liked him, but knew you would never listen to me about him. Maybe now you'll accept he was a horrible person and none of his words were true.*

Hayley retrieved a folder and placed it in front of the man in the center of the front table. "New evidence for you to consider, Mr. Bailey. It's the medical records from Dr. Hughes and the warrant for Dewi Lewis's arrest, signed by Rhydian Griffiths."

The man scanned the documents and passed them to one of his colleagues. "The warrant was approved by the DDA and still stands. As such, as soon as Dewi Lewis appears, he'll be handed over to Snowridge's custody." He glanced at Madalena at the other table. "Do you still wish to use him as your key character witness?"

The dragonwoman shook her head. "No. But my claim on my grandsons still stands. I won't let that male neglect and kill them."

Trahern growled, but Grace shook her head a fraction. He rarely showed his temper, and he needed to get himself under control.

The man gestured toward Hayley. "Then continue stating your case, Ms. Beckett."

And as Hayley interviewed each of the dragonmen from Snowridge, Trahern had trouble believing their words were true.

They lauded his intelligence, his willingness to help other doctors with research, and how dedicated he'd been to his patients back on Snowridge. How he'd given lectures to children at the school, and helped a few better understand chemistry or biology. Or, how he'd given advice to the teachers on how to handle another student who'd shown similar habits to him and how to engage him better.

So many things he'd forgotten about and had dismissed as inconsequential.

His dragon spoke again. *It's because you never took praise or compliments to heart, always believing the worst of people thanks to our father's influence.*

Had he really allowed his father's hateful words to color everything?

Once Hayley finished questioning the Snowridge males, she called more witnesses from Stonefire, and even Dr. Scarlett Turner. Antony Holbrook had wanted to come, too, but his position needed to remain in a fuzzy gray area, which meant staying out of the limelight. But the human male had pledged Iris could testify, if needed.

However, as Hayley attempted to call yet another person to vouch for him, the human in the middle of the table up front, Mr. Bailey, put up a hand. "I think we've heard enough. And since Mrs. Silva has dropped her only witness, we have enough information to make our decision." He glanced down one side of the table, and then the other. Each nodded. "Those in favor of allowing Grace and Trahern Lewis to keep sole custody, raise your hand." All five hands went up. "The decision is made. If you wish to have visitation rights for holidays or on a prearranged schedule, feel free to submit another request. For now, this matter is closed."

As the five humans stood, Trahern somehow managed to rise, too. However, he still tried to process what had just happened.

Custody, yes, they'd been awarded full custody. However, he still didn't understand why so many people had come to his defense.

His dragon spoke up. *Dragon clans have each other's backs in the UK. Maybe not everywhere, but here, they rally around any of their members who are loyal and good and true.*

Grace hugged him, and he awkwardly patted her back as his supporters all walked up to them. He met Rhydian's eye, and asked, "Is it true? About why my father ran?"

"I wouldn't lie about it, Trahern. I tried to tell you, but you were very good at avoiding people. And then you went to Stonefire, and well." Rhydian shrugged. "But as soon as we heard about this case, I knew I had to come in person and share the information." He put out a hand to shake. "Please visit Snowridge anytime you like, we'd be happy to have you."

For once, he didn't hesitate to shake Rhydian's hand and drop it. "Thank you."

Grace stood at his side, her arm around his waist, and leaned against him. "Thank you, all of you, for helping us to keep our boys."

As his mate chatted with everyone, he was content to hold his female and merely study the people around the room.

Someone entered, someone he didn't know. And yet the set of the male's eyes and nose were similar to Madalena Silva's, probably a relation.

The dragonman pushed people aside and headed right for them. "Where are they, Grace?" He shouted. "They're mine, you little bitch. And I'll take you, if need be, to get what's owed."

Without thinking, Trahern pushed Grace behind him and walked up to the male. The male's eyes flashed as he growled, "Get out of my way, you geeky bastard."

Before his dragon could speak, Trahern raised a fist and punched the man in the face.

Pain radiated up his arm, but the male dropped to

the ground. As he shook his hand, he blinked and tried to understand why he'd done that.

His dragon snorted. *The bastard deserved it, that's why. Well done.*

Rhydian, Wren, Kai Sutherland, and a few other Protectors stood around the unconscious dragonman. However, a human DDA bailiff came through. After checking the unconscious male's ID, he stated, "This is Afonso Silva, who is wanted by the DDA." The human looked at Trahern. "Since he's alive, and you helped us apprehend the dragonman, I won't press charges, Dr. Lewis. Now, if a few of you lads would help me get this dragonman to a holding cell, I'd appreciate it. He's a heavy bastard, for sure."

As the Protectors hauled off the male—none too gently—Grace placed a hand on his cheek. "Are you sure you're okay? You didn't break your hand, did you?"

"No, it's not broken, but it bloody hurts. I don't understand why someone would find punching people fun."

She smiled, kissed him, and then allowed Dr. Turner to assess his hand and confirm it wasn't broken.

Once he was alone—well, as alone as he could be in a full room—with Grace, he searched her gaze for signs of anger or disappointment.

But all he saw was love and approval. He blurted, "You're happy I hit him, aren't you?"

"Maybe I shouldn't be, but I rather enjoyed watching him drop to the ground." She leaned against his chest, and Trahern wrapped his arms around his mate. She continued, "Let's go home, Trahern. Home to our boys." She lowered her voice. "And home so I can finally claim you as mine."

Both man and beast approved, and Trahern did his best to get them out of the room and heading back to Stonefire as quickly as possible.

Because he was done waiting. He wanted his mate in his bed. And soon.

Chapter Twenty-Two

Even though Grace was thrilled that the custody case was over, the next twenty or so hours were some of the longest of her life. They'd arrived back on Stonefire late, and then they'd had to take care of Eli and Eddie. And after that, they'd had just enough energy to eat something and crash on the bed to sleep.

At least Hayley and Dawn had both volunteered to watch the boys overnight so that Trahern could finally claim her as his mate in all ways. It was strange because, a few months before, Grace would've hesitated to let her twins out of her sight. However, both women had done so much to help her, and she trusted them now.

And so, with her boys safely in the care of her friends, Grace currently waited in the bedroom. She played with the belt on her robe, trying not to be nervous, which only made her anxiety worse. She worried that Trahern had built everything up in his mind, and she couldn't live up to his standards.

Stop it. He wants you, and that's it. You have the rest of your lives to get things exactly right in this arena.

Still, she continued fingering her robe until Trahern suddenly appeared in the doorway and everything else melted away. With a smile, she dashed to him and crashed against his chest.

His arms wrapped around her, and he chuckled—actually chuckled—before saying, "You're impatient."

She met his gaze. "And you're not?"

His pupils flashed a few times, and he groaned. "My dragon is extremely impatient." He raised a hand to cup her cheek. "But don't worry, he won't rush me. You're too important to us, and this is something I want to remember forever."

"But you always remember everything."

"Perhaps, but memories of you and the boys are my favorite."

She melted against him and grinned. "You've gotten rather smooth, haven't you?"

"I speak the truth, nothing else."

As they stared at each other for a few beats, Grace's heart raced, and love for her dragonman rushed through her. It was time, long past time, to finally claim his body in addition to his heart.

Well, his cock, at any rate.

She kissed him, and Trahern didn't hesitate or tease. He merely devoured her mouth, exploring with his tongue as if it were the first time all over again, and running his hands down her back to cup her bum.

The feel of his large, warm hands kneading her flesh made her moan into his mouth. She was already wet, and she was as impatient as a randy virgin.

She broke the kiss. "Tell me you're ready, Trahern. Please say you are."

He chuckled again—she'd never heard him do that with anyone else, and she treasured it each time—and replied, "You can feel that I'm aroused, Grace. So yes, I'm ready."

She cupped his face in her hands and shook her head. "That's not what I mean. I don't want you to be nervous or hesitant or have the urge to run. I want you, Trahern, but I love you enough to wait, if you need it."

His face softened. He kissed her and then murmured, "I love you for many reasons, Grace Lewis. But I've been ready for a while. This first time might be rather quick, though, as Blake and Gregor have teased me ever since I discussed wanting to have intercourse with you."

She smiled. "Well, I've heard dragonmen recover quickly, so we can practice as many times as you like to build up some stamina."

He lightly swatted her arse—she'd told him once she liked it, and as always, he made sure to do everything she liked—and said, "We'll see. Now, take off your clothes, Grace. I want to see your lovely body before anything else."

Grace stepped back a few paces and untied her robe before dropping it to the floor. As always, Trahern's gaze turned heated as his pupils flashed. He always made her feel beautiful and desirable, and he would only ever want her.

Wetness rushed to her core as his gaze lingered on her breasts before settling on the juncture of her thighs.

He wasn't even touching her, and she was the most aroused she'd ever been in her life.

Her voice was hoarse to her own ears as stated, "Now, take off your clothes."

Trahern didn't hesitate to tug off his top, trousers, and underwear. He didn't even bother to fold them in a pile like normal, but instead headed straight for her, pulled her close and kissed her.

Their kiss was passionate and demanding and full of how much they wanted each other.

Soon she felt the back of her legs hit the bed, and Trahern broke the kiss. "Lie back, Grace. Maybe later you can try some of the positions I found in a book, with you on top. However, I want to be on top and in charge this first time."

She nodded, understanding that he needed to be in control for this given his past, and lay back. After spreading her legs, Trahern settled between them. The feel of his hot skin against hers made her arch her back and rub her center against his hard cock. "Trahern."

He kissed her at the same time as his fingers found her clit and strummed in the rhythm she liked. She wanted to tell him she didn't have to orgasm first this time, that she wanted this memory to be special for him. However, soon she was close, digging her nails into his back, and pleasure crashed over her. She cried out his name as wave after wave of ecstasy came over her.

By the time her orgasm finally ended, she met Trahern's eyes again. He smiled rather smugly. Something else he only ever did with her.

"Are you going to just stare at me smiling or do you want to actually have sex for the first time?"

"I am a patient male, Grace. I could make you come again first."

She traced his lips with a finger, first the top and then the bottom, before whispering, "Claim me, Trahern. Make me your mate in all ways."

Letting her love for him shine in her eyes, she waited.

Trahern's heart raced as his cock throbbed. Grace was naked and under him, and all he had to do was enter her.

But for a split second, he hesitated. Maybe he should make her orgasm again.

His dragon spoke up. *Stop stalling. This is Grace, our mate, our love. She's wet and swollen and ready.*

He met Grace's eyes again. Full of desire and something softer, maybe love, he relaxed a fraction before replying to his beast. *As long as you keep your vow to give me some time after, before you claim Grace.*

Of course I will, as long as you keep your promise to share.

Grace touched his cheek, but before she could say anything, he kissed her. She opened without hesitation, and he lost himself in her heat and taste and the way she threaded her fingers through his hair.

He continued kissing her as he positioned himself at her entrance. Then he pushed slowly, until he was inside her to the hilt.

Instead of the urge to run or retreat, he groaned. Being inside Grace just felt...right. She gripped him just the right way, and combined with her kisses, he started moving his hips, wanting more. Much more.

Finally breaking the kiss, Trahern held Grace's gaze with his own. Unlike with everyone else, her eyes didn't make him uncomfortable. He knew the dark brown depths nearly as well as his own, and they were home.

More than a place, wherever his mate was, that was his home.

The urge to claim her and fill her coursed through him, and he increased his pace. He wanted to last longer, tried his best, but she was so warm and wet and gripped him perfectly that he couldn't. And with a growl, he stilled and released inside her.

Any doubts about her being his true mate fled as she instantly orgasmed, gripping and releasing his cock, prolonging his own pleasure.

When she'd finally wrung every last drop from him, Trahern collapsed atop his mate. He knew he should roll over and stop crushing her, but he was too happy and sated and tired.

Only after Grace started playing with the hair at the nape of his neck did he muster the strength to roll to the side. He hated leaving her body, but pulled her close against his chest. The contact helped calm him a fraction.

Just a bit, though, as his dragon paced his mind. *When is it my turn?*

Soon. Just give me a few minutes.

With a harrumph, his dragon continued pacing.

Grace's voice brought him back to the present. "So how was it? Your first time?"

By now, Trahern knew most of Grace's tells. And the slightly lower volume of her voice meant she was uncertain or nervous.

He tilted her head up to meet his gaze before he kissed her and whispered, "Bloody amazing."

She smiled, and it stirred both his heart and his cock again.

"I'm glad. I know that's kind of awkward, and not sexy or romantic, but it's more important to me that you enjoy sex because I'd rather like to do it again."

He rolled her onto her back, kissed her, and replied, "I will always want to do it with you, Grace. But it will be shared with my dragon. I hope that's still okay."

"I'm ready for him whenever he is. I love all of you, Trahern. Nothing will change that."

It was still hard for him to believe someone cared for him. And yet, as Grace smiled at him, with her eyes soft and tender, he knew she did.

His dragon spoke up. *It's my turn. Warn her I want to be in charge and how dragons like it.*

You'll give me control again when you're done?

Yes, we're past the stage of wrestling it from one another. Grace is ours, and we share.

So, no pull for a frenzy?

No, but our past is different, and we were distant for a long time. I think even emotionally we might still never understand one another. However, Grace is ours. We work together. All will be well.

Maybe later he'd ask his dragon for further clarification, but for now, Trahern focused back on Grace. After tracing her cheek, he said, "My dragon wants his turn. It'll be a bit different, from what he's told me and others say."

She smiled. "I've heard plenty from the other human mates, and I'm more than a bit curious. I'm ready whenever he is."

"Are you sure?"

After kissing him, she replied, "Yes, I'm ready for your dragon."

His beast growled. *She's ready. Don't fight me.*

Battling the urge to hesitate, he retreated to the back

of his mind. He needed to trust his dragon completely, or they would never form a close bond.

And while he had Grace and the boys, he wanted that with his dragon, too.

As his beast took control, he said, *We're on our way, and won't go back to how it used to be. I won't let it.*

Neither will I.

Good. Now, let me claim our female.

With his dragon in control of their human form, Trahern watched to see what happened next.

Grace was more curious than anxious about Trahern's dragon half. From all she'd heard, the sex would be rougher but still fantastic.

Although she was more curious about what his beast would say while in charge. Sometimes, she wished there was a way to talk with his dragon more often, without the human half being the middleman.

However, as soon as Trahern's pupils turned to slits and stayed that way, she pushed all other thoughts out of her mind.

Trahern's voice was deeper than normal, and sent a thrill through her body, in a good way, as he stated, "You're my mate. I'm claiming you. Now."

She spread her arms and legs wide, but his dragon surprised her by flipping her over and raising her hips up.

Then without preamble, he entered her. At this angle, Trahern's cock filled her up more, and rubbed against a spot inside her that drove her wild as he moved.

Because his dragon didn't hesitate or say pretty words or take things slow. Oh, no, he moved his hips quickly, keeping her in place, and she moaned into the bed as she felt herself getting closer and closer.

Never close enough, though.

Then she felt fingers on her clit, and with a few firm strokes, pleasure shot through her as she came. She'd barely started to come down again when Trahern's dragon stilled, released inside her, and another orgasm crashed down, intensifying the pulses and pleasure to the point it was nearly overwhelming, bordering between pain and bliss.

However, as Trahern's dragon pressed his front against her back and hot breath danced against her neck, her body started to relax, hovering between an orgasm ending and the world coming back into focus.

She was about to collapse onto the bed when cool air suddenly hit her back. In the next second, she was cuddled against Trahern's side again as he kissed the top of her head. "Are you okay?"

His voice was back to its normal timbre, and a quick check revealed his pupils to be round. "So your dragon doesn't mess about, does he? Done and gone."

Trahern frowned. "I did tell you dragons were different."

Reaching up, she smoothed the lines on his forehead.

"I was teasing, Trahern. Dawn and Hayley both warned about how a dragon half might be quick, and sometimes that's nice. In fact, having two halves to one person, and different approaches to sex, makes for never getting bored."

He visibly relaxed a fraction, but remained silent as he stroked her back with his hand. Not wanting him to retreat, she asked, "So what's this book you talked about? The one with sexual positions?"

She swore his cheeks pinkened a fraction. "Blake gave it to me so he wouldn't have to talk about it."

"I'm interested in seeing it later. Maybe even your dragon will find a few positions to try out."

His gaze finally met hers again, and his pupils flashed a few times. "He's not against the idea."

She moved to straddle Trahern's hips and pressed her hands to his chest. After leaning down to kiss him, she whispered, "For now, I have an idea about how to try it next." She rubbed her pussy against his cock, and Trahern moaned. "If you're up for it. Dragon-shifters are supposed to have more stamina, but if you need some time to recover..."

His fingers tickled her side, and she laughed. He flipped her under him again, kissed her, and then murmured, "You know how I become fixated on things. I think making love with you will be my new favorite one."

She touched his cheek. "Making love, huh?"

"Yes. I love you, Grace. And I always will."

Grace expected skepticism to course through her, but the tender look in his eyes, complete with flashing pupils, and the way he then kissed her slowly, as if she were the most treasured thing in the world, made her realize she believed him. "I'm glad you mated me, Trahern. I love you, and I look forward to growing old with you and our boys."

"You three are my family, Grace. And I will always take care of you."

"Kiss me, Trahern. For now, just kiss me."

And so he did, before claiming her over and over again until Grace fell asleep in the arms of the man she loved, looking forward to a future she never would've imagined having until coming to Stonefire.

Epilogue

Seven Years Later

Trahern cradled his baby daughter in his lap as he watched Eli and Eddie play cricket with some of the other children on Stonefire. They were on the same team as Jasper and Theo—Dawn and Blake's twin sons—and struggled against the opposing team's bowler, Lucy Hartley-Gray.

Every time Lucy threw—or bowled—the ball, the boys were a half-second too late in swinging to make contact.

He'd tried to teach them how to time their swings. But seven-year-old boys weren't as interested in physics and mathematical equations as he was.

His daughter, Ceri, squirmed, and he focused on

her. She was nearly a year old now and had been frustrated she couldn't play with her brothers.

However, Grace said Ceri was a "daddy's girl," meaning she would calm down for him and no one else. So he'd taken her and described the physics of hitting a ball as she sucked her thumb and stared at him.

By the time he'd finished, the game was over. Lucy's team had won, and even though Eddie and Eli shook hands like gentlemen, they dragged their feet, their pupils flashing, and muttered as they approached Grace and Dawn's table for drinks and snacks.

Trahern stood, holding Ceri against his chest with her facing out—she was curious about everything, and Trahern thought she might end up a doctor or scientist like him—and headed over to his family. While he wished Emily hadn't returned to Clan Seahaven last week with her mate since Grace and the boys had gotten along with her and her sons, he understood her home was in Scotland and not here.

At least he liked Emily's mate, so he didn't have to worry about her.

His dragon spoke up. *Emily is happy, as are we. She invited us up to Seahaven for the holidays.*

I know. But she's like my sister, and Grace likes her too. Distance makes it difficult to establish times with Emily, her boys, and her mate.

But we have lots of friends, both here and in Wales, as well as with many of Antony Holbrook's team.

It was still strange for him to accept that fact, given his childhood.

However, as Grace caught his eye and beamed at him, he forgot about everything but his mate and children. As soon as he reached the table, Eli sighed and said, "Please don't go over more equations, Dad. I know my swing is off, but right now, I just want to avoid Lucy and her team."

He nodded over his son's shoulder. "They're right there. And Lucy isn't arrogant. If you ask her, she'll teach you better than I can."

Eddie slapped his brother's shoulder—even older, they were nearly identical, except Eddie kept his curly hair short and Eli liked it longer and braided into rows by his mother—and said, "You want to avoid her because you fancy her."

"I don't fancy her!"

"You do."

Sensing they would keep arguing, he merely stated, "It takes a strong person to ask for help, I know. But will you benefit more from being stubborn, or by finding a way to improve something, no matter how difficult it is?"

Eli sighed even deeper. "I know, Dad. You're right. I'll ask Lucy in a bit, but for now, I'm starving."

Grace finally jumped in as she handed the boys a snack. "When aren't you?"

Eli stuck out his tongue, and Grace laughed. Then she leaned over and kissed Eli's forehead before he could run away.

"Mu-um!"

Grace shrugged. "Your parents love you, and we don't hide it."

She then kissed Eddie's cheek, and he merely grunted.

Eli glanced at Trahern. "You're not going to kiss me too, are you, Dad? Please don't."

Trahern had been learning about young dragon boy pride, although still struggled to understand why it was embarrassing to find ways to improve or show affection for those you cared about.

Still, he readjusted Ceri and held her out. "Kiss your sister and then we won't kiss you anymore in public today."

Dragging his feet, Eli moved until he could kiss his sister's cheek. Eddie did the same without asking, and then the boys darted off to the other team, and the rest of the children followed. Dawn and Grace shared a look before Grace came over to him. She kissed him quickly, then their daughter, and Trahern moved Ceri to one arm and wrapped the other around his mate's waist.

He murmured, "I love you, Grace. And you, Ceri."

His mate met his gaze, her eyes full of love, and she replied, "I love you more, Trahern."

The urge to argue the point receded as Grace leaned against him and placed a hand over his arm, hugging both him and Ceri. His dragon hummed, and Trahern held his mate and daughter close, watching as his sons played in the distance, and couldn't believe he had a family of his own to love, and who loved him back.

Author's Note

Thanks for reading Grace and Trahern's story! This one was a bit different for a few reasons, but Trahern is our first neurodivergent hero. Creating what that means for his dragon half was interesting and a little difficult, but I think we got there in the end. :) The human spectrum is pretty broad, and while I've learned a lot from my good friend who has two neurodivergent children, as well as from my time subbing regularly for nonverbal autistic students years ago, I am no expert. Trahern is a fictional character, complete with an inner dragon, so I think his experience is unique and please don't judge him by human standards!

As for what story is next, I'm still working that out. I'm sure you noticed a few set-ups/continuations in this story! It'll probably be 1) Marianna and Brodie's story, 2) Dr. Emily Davies' story on Clan Seahaven, or 3) Katrina "Trina" Lau (Nikki's half-sister) on Stonefire. Those are the next three stories, but I'm still deciding which order they go in! I'm actually working on my next Dark Lords of London book (*Vampires' Shared Bride*) first, so the next dragon book should be out in April or May, I think. :)

As always, I thank not only my readers but also the people who helped to make this book a reality:

- My beta readers Iliana, Sabrina, Ashley, and Amy are all amazing and help the final book shine. Not only do they catch any lingering typos, they also point out the minor inconsistencies I probably would've never noticed myself.

Thanks again for reading! And while waiting for my next dragon book, I hope you'll give my other paranormal romance series, Dark Lords of London, a try. It's a paranormal time travel series with vampires, shifters, and fae witches. The first book is called *Vampire's Modern Bride*.

Until next time, I'll see you at the end of the next book!

About the Author

Jessie Donovan has sold over half a million books, has given away hundreds of thousands more to readers for free, and has even hit the *NY Times* and *USA Today* bestseller lists. She is best known for her dragon-shifter series, but also writes about magic users, aliens, and even has a crazy romantic comedy series set in Scotland. When not reading a book, attempting to tame her yard, or traipsing around some foreign country on a shoestring, she can often be found interacting with her readers on Facebook. She lives near Seattle, where, yes, it rains a lot but it also makes everything green.

Visit her website at: www.JessieDonovan.com